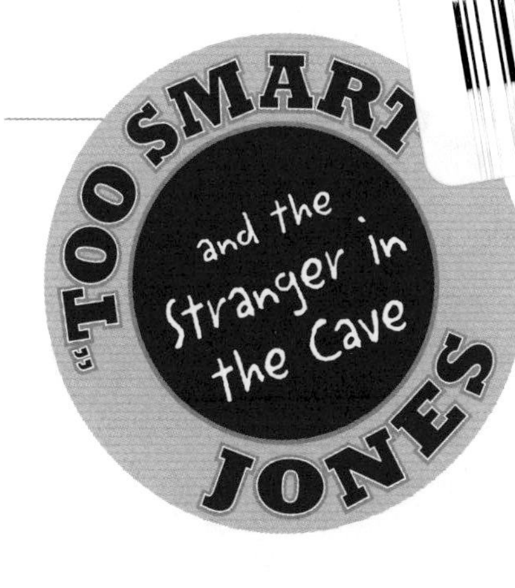

A GILBERT MORRIS MYSTERY

MOODY PRESS
CHICAGO

ISBN: 0-8024-4029-0

1 3 5 7 9 10 8 6 4 2

Printed in the United States of America

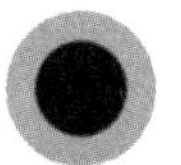

Contents

OAKWOOD

A New Mystery for Too Smart Jones

Juliet Jones picked up another rock. As she did, she heard her brother grunt with satisfaction. Juliet turned around to look at him. "What did you find?"

Joe Jones was ten. He had red hair and blue eyes, just like his dad, and he was tall and gangly. He wore a pair of faded jeans today and a shirt that had once been bright red. It was now faded to reddish brown. He held up a stone. "You see that?"

"Of course, I see it. I'm not blind."

"You know what it is?"

"It's a rock."

"I know that!" Joe snapped. "What kind of rock?"

Juliet fumbled in the pocket of her blue shirt and put on her glasses. "It's a—a red rock," she said.

"And they call you Too Smart Jones!" Joe sniffed. "It's an *igneous* rock! I thought everybody knew that!"

Juliet knew better than to argue with Joe when he was in this mood. She happened to be very good at schoolwork—so good that her nickname was "Too Smart Jones." Joe was not as quick at books as she was. But he was smart about anything mechanical. He was always tearing things apart and trying to put them back together. He also worked on many inventions. Some of them seemed absolutely crazy to Juliet.

"So what's an igneous rock?" she asked. She listened as Joe explained the difference between igneous rocks and sedimentary rocks. She could tell he liked explaining things to her. Usually she had to explain things to *him*.

When he finished, she shook her head. "You're so good at identifying rocks, Joe. They all just look like rocks to me."

Joe beamed at his sister. Then he said suddenly, "You know what?"

"What?"

"We haven't had an argument in over two hours."

Juliet laughed aloud. "I think that must be a record. You want to try for three?"

"Naw," Joe said. "It's too dull." He pulled Juliet's cap down over her eyes. It was a cap with the donkey Eeyore on it. She had bought it at Disney World, and she was very proud of it.

"Watch what you're doing, Joe! Let go of my cap!"

"You need a good cap like this one." Joe tipped his. It was bright green with OAKWOOD on the front.

"Everybody's got one of those!" Juliet said. She took off her glasses and put them back in her pocket.

They were collecting rock samples for a school project. Since they were homeschooled, their schedule was easy to follow. They worked on their studies in the morning, did their chores after lunch, and then they were free to play. Today, they'd decided to spend their afternoon free time out in the woods.

They roamed among the trees for a while longer. Then Juliet said, "It's getting kind of late." She hefted the bag that hung from a strap around her neck. "This thing's getting heavy. We've got enough rocks for one day."

"Let's just try over there," Joe said. "See that ravine? I bet if we climbed down there, we'd find lots of different rocks. That's an old riverbed, I think."

Juliet would rather have gone on home. But Joe had had such a good day that she decided to please him. "All right, but after that we've got to go, Joe."

"Aw, you girls are always wimping out!"

"Sure. Let's do it."

The entrance to the cavern was so low that they had to stoop to go in. Joe turned on his penlight right away, and the tiny light pierced the dimness. It was cool inside, and the cave turned out to be high enough to walk in.

Soon the sides of the cave widened out, and Joe whispered, "It's getting bigger. See? I'll bet it gets as big as Mammoth Cave."

Juliet stayed close as they moved along. And then she looked down and saw something interesting. "Look, Joe."

"What is it?"

Juliet picked up a piece of paper. "Shine your light here," she said. When Joe did, she exclaimed, "Well, the pirates were here not long ago. Look at this."

"It's a . . . Snickers bar wrapper."

"That's right. And I'll bet that Bluebeard, the famous pirate, didn't eat Snickers bars."

"Aw, shoot!" Joe complained. "And here I thought we'd found a pirate cave."

"I think it's just an old mine of some kind," Juliet said. "Isn't that part of a track over there?"

They looked closely at some old boards that lay in order.

"Looks like it," Joe said. "The tracks are all gone—like maybe somebody took them. Just the wood that held them is left."

"We'd better go back, Joe," Juliet said nervously. “There might be bats in here, and bats sometimes have rabies.”

But Joe said stoutly, “Not yet. Just a little farther.”

They had gone just a few more steps when Joe’s penlight picked up something. “Whoa,” he said softly, “look what we found.”

They edged forward.

“It’s a sleeping bag,” Juliet said.

“Somebody’s been living here!”

“And here’s some canned food—and a backpack.”

Juliet squinted at the cave floor. “Looks like there’s been a fire over here . . .”

Indeed, Juliet thought, the cave was inhabited.

Then she saw some drawings on the stone wall. She went to look at one. “Shine your light on this, Joe,” she said.

Joe held the light steady, and together they looked at the picture of a large grasshopper.

“It looks just like a grasshopper,” Juliet said.

“Yeah, and look at this picture of a dog. You can almost hear him bark.”

“Somebody’s been trying to make the cave pretty.” Then Juliet turned away, saying, “Let’s see what else is in here.”

Right away, Joe picked up the backpack and began to open it.

“Don’t do that, Joe!”

"Why not?"

"Because it's not yours. How would you like it if someone went through your backpack?"

Joe hesitated, but then he shook his head. "I want to find out who's living here." He suddenly laughed. "You're the one that always sees a mystery behind every tree. This time *I'm* the one looking for a mystery."

And suddenly Juliet's great curiosity overcame her. She leaned forward and said, "What's in there?"

"Well, here's a toothbrush. Some toothpaste. And here's a comb and some soap . . ."

"What's underneath? Clothes?"

"Looks like some pants and a couple of T-shirts."

They went through the contents of the backpack carefully. And then something fell out of the shirt that Juliet was folding to put back. She picked it up.

"Let me have your light, Joe."

Joe handed over the penlight.

"It's a picture," Juliet said.

Joe leaned closer, and they stared at the photo she held. It was a snapshot of two girls. The bigger one looked to be a little older than Juliet and Joe.

"Look on the back and see if anything's written there," Joe advised.

Juliet looked. "No. Nothing there. We'd better put it back just where it was."

Carefully they repacked the things they had taken out of the backpack.

As Juliet followed Joe back toward the cave entrance, her mind was busy. *Who is staying in this cave? Why is he staying here? And who are the two girls in that picture?*

"Juliet," Joe said all of a sudden, "I can just hear your mind cranking."

"What are you talking about?"

"I know what you're doing. You're trying to make some big mystery out of this."

"Well, it is kind of a mystery, isn't it?"

"No. It's not a mystery. Somebody has been camping out in this cave. That's all."

Juliet did not answer. She just followed Joe out into the fading daylight. She blinked and said, "It's late. We'd better get home."

"I guess you're right this time," he agreed.

As they tramped back along the old streambed and then through the woods toward the park, Juliet was doing exactly what Joe had accused her of doing. She had a good imagination, and now she had another mystery to solve.

Maybe it's not a pirate cave, she thought, shifting the weight of the rocks. *But I'm going to find out who's been in it!*

Juliet and Jenny

Joe might be better at finding rocks, but it was Juliet who enjoyed getting them ready for display. She sat in their classroom watching the rock tumbler as it went around and around. The tumbler had been their father's when he was a boy.

The rock tumbler itself was nothing but a container that ran on a small electric motor. It turned very slowly and made a slight humming noise. When rocks were tumbled inside, the churning around made them smooth.

"This batch ought to be done now," she said. She looked over at Joe. "Let's take the rocks out and see what they look like."

"Just a minute. I'm about to get my new invention finished."

"What is that you're working on now?" Juliet asked as she unplugged the rock tumbler.

"It's a burglar alarm."

"We never have burglars around here, Joe."

"Well, we might have. And if one of them does come, he's going to get a surprise. Let's do the rocks, and then I'll show you how it works."

Juliet unscrewed the end of the tumbler and took out the rocks.

"Here. Let me wipe them off," Joe said. He reached for a white cloth on a shelf and began polishing the stones. "Boy!" he said. "These are really something, aren't they?"

"They sure are. You wouldn't know they were just plain old rocks when we put them in there."

The rocks, after being tumbled for such a long time, were indeed beautiful. Some were dark green with light green streaks. One of them was a beautiful sky blue. And still a third was bright yellow against a gray background.

Joe held up the green rock and admired it. "This one will look good in a display," he said.

"And this one will, too." Juliet picked up the largest of the rocks, which was a bright, purplish color. "We could arrange them by color instead of by the kinds of rocks they are."

She knew that Joe was not particularly interested in the display, though. What he liked was going out and finding the rocks.

"Any way you want to do it will be fine with me," he said.

It was Juliet's job to put white labels on the rocks. As she went to work, she grinned at Joe and said, "I guess I can call you the rock king."

He leaned back. "That's me. King of the rocks."

After all the stones were labeled and mounted, Joe said, "Now let me show you my foolproof, guaranteed burglar alarm."

Juliet was a little worried. Joe's inventions were sometimes dangerous. After the accident when he had used some firecracker powder to make a rocket, their father had strictly forbidden the use of any dangerous chemicals.

"You don't have any gunpowder in this, do you, Joe?"

"No. And I wish I could, but you know what Dad said. Anyhow, here's the way it works, and this idea is a dilly!"

Joe went to the window, where he had attached some wires. There was a spring that went to a can at the top of the window.

"It's like this," he said. "When the burglar opens the window, that releases the catch on this can. You see it up there?"

"I see. Then what happens?"

"Well, when he steps in, he hits this little tiny wire. You can't even see it, it's so fine. See how fine it is?"

"Well, it would be dark, so I don't guess he could see it. What does that do?"

"It triggers this spring, and just when he's

halfway through—" Joe moved quickly, showing her how the invention worked "—it turns the can upside down. And that's the end of the burglar."

"Why? What's in the can? Water?"

"Water? That wouldn't do any good!" Joe snorted. "No, I'm going to use some chloroform."

"Chloroform!"

"Yeah. The chloroform will go down over the robber's head, and it will put him to sleep. And this other wire sets off this whistle. See, I got it attached right over here. Now I'll show you how it all works."

"You better not, Joe!"

"Aw, don't be such a wimp!"

Joe confidently opened the window. Then he winked at her. "Don't worry. I got the can filled with water this time instead of chloroform. So there's no problem."

Juliet watched him reach out and touch the wire. The can above the window turned upside down. The water splashed on the window sill below, and at the same time an ear-splitting noise sounded.

"Joe, what *is* that?"

"It's my burglar alarm. Isn't it neat?" He fumbled with the alarm, trying to turn it off.

Suddenly the door flew open, and Mrs. Jones came running in. "What are you *doing?*"

She had obviously been busy with housework, for she wore an apron. "Shut that thing off!"

Joe gave his mother a startled look. Then he fumbled some more until the high-pitched, screaming siren settled down to a low hum and went off.

Their mother said, "What *was* that?"

"It's my new burglar alarm, Mom. I'm going to put one on every window."

"You are not going to put that thing on *any* window, and I want it disconnected right now!"

"But, Mom," Joe protested, "what if a burglar comes in at night and steals all of our stuff?"

"This is the second floor—and besides, there's nothing in here that's valuable."

"Nothing valuable!" Joe cried. "Why, all of my inventions are in here!"

"And all of our displays, Mom!" Juliet added. "They might steal our rock collection."

"Then you'll have to go make another one. What if that thing went off in the middle of the night? It would scare everybody to death."

Both Joe and Juliet knew better than to argue with their mother when she was in this kind of mood. But Joe could be heard mumbling, "I'll bet Thomas Edison didn't get treated like this when he invented stuff."

"I heard that!" Mrs. Jones said, but she was smiling. She came over and ruffled his hair. "I didn't mean to yell at you, Joe. I'm very proud of the way you've learned to invent things. Someday you're going to invent something so wonderful that I'll point at you and say, 'That's my son, Joseph Jones, the great inventor!'"

Juliet laughed. "He'll probably invent an automatic egg cracker."

"I already did that. It worked too," Joe said.

Juliet and Joe then had to go over their schoolwork with their mother. When they had first learned that they were to be taken out of public school, they thought that having their mother for a teacher would be a breeze. They'd quickly learned that Mrs. Jones was as tough as any teacher in any school anywhere.

When they finished, and before Juliet started downstairs for lunch, she picked up the extension phone in her room. She dialed a number. "Jenny, is that you?"

"Yes. What are you doing, Juliet?"

"Oh, nothing much. Joe and I just finished our schoolwork. What are you doing?"

They played the "What are you doing?" game for a while. Then they talked about other things.

Finally Juliet said, "Jenny, something exciting happened in the woods yesterday."

"What was that?"

"Joe and I found a mysterious cave."

At once Jenny became very cautious. "You didn't go in it, did you?"

"Sure, we went in it. What's the good of finding a cave if you don't go exploring?"

"I've heard some bad stories about kids going into caves. Some caves have old mine shafts that go straight down. Kids fall into them and get killed."

"We were real careful, and Joe had his flashlight. But guess what? Someone is *living* in this cave, Jenny."

"You mean you saw somebody?"

"Well, no. We didn't actually see them, but we found lots of their stuff." Juliet waved her free hand while she talked, describing what she and Joe had found. Then she said, "Jenny, let's us go out there, and I'll show it to you."

"Uh . . . all right. I guess so. We can look at the *outside* of it."

"When do you want to go?"

"I can't go until day after tomorrow."

"All right. Saturday morning it is. Let's go real early, and we'll pack a lunch. We might want to set up surveillance."

"What's that?"

"Oh, you know. It means what the police say when they hide and watch for criminals."

"Juliet, do you think there's a *criminal* living in that cave?"

"Oh, I don't think so. But you can't be too careful. I'll bring my binoculars. We can take turns looking at him."

"Well . . . all right. But I'm a little bit scared of things like this."

Jenny White was shy and timid, but Juliet knew she really liked it when Juliet was working on a case and took her along.

"OK. And we can go inside and look in the backpack again, too. That won't hurt anything. We might find a book or a driver's license or something else to help us."

"What if the man catches us?"

"He won't. We'll be careful. Well, I got to run now. I'll see you Saturday morning. Bye-bye."

Detective Work

Juliet spent a lot of time writing in her journal. She kept it carefully hidden in the bottom drawer of her dresser, where she also kept many things that Joe called "just junk." She remembered a story in which a man had to hide a letter. He knew that people would be searching his room, so finally he put it right on top of a table—where nobody would think to look. *That was smart,* Juliet had thought. *I'll put my journal under this junk, and no one will ever think to look for it here.*

Juliet enjoyed writing in her journal. It had a hard cover and a beautiful picture of hunting dogs chasing birds. It looked like a real book, but it was a "nothing" book. There was nothing on the pages.

Joe seemed to have forgotten the cave, but Juliet had not. And in the journal she wrote down all the questions about the mysterious cave that she could think of. By the time Saturday came, she had filled two pages.

Every Saturday at the Jones house, they had pancakes for breakfast. Juliet had learned to make them. Her dad said, when she brought them from the griddle and put them down, "Sweetheart, you make pancakes as good as your mother's."

"Thank you, Dad," Juliet said. She loved it when her father said nice things about her. She sat down, thinking, *What a nice dad I have!* She looked at his tall, strong form and red hair and blue eyes. She grinned at her mother. "I'm glad you picked a good-looking man for my dad," she said.

"Yeah, it'd be awful to have an ugly father," Joe spoke up. "Besides, I get all my good looks from him."

"You're not going to get any awards for being humble," his mother admonished him.

"I can't help it, Mom," Joe teased. "Every time I look in the mirror I think what a handsome boy I am. And I owe it all to you, Dad."

"Well, I'm glad Juliet took after her mother," Mr. Jones said.

"I don't think she looks much like me at all."

"Sure she does. Her eyes are just like yours. That's why I fell in love with your mother, Juliet. She had those sparkling eyes, and you've got them, too."

"I just wish I could see without glasses. I don't care how much they sparkle."

Joe crammed a big bite of pancake into his mouth. "Aw, you like to wear glasses," he said.

"I can't understand a word you're saying," Juliet said. "Don't talk with your mouth full."

"And don't *get* your mouth so full!" Mr. Jones said.

Joe managed to swallow his bite and immediately forked three more pieces. "Seems I'm getting a lot of advice on eating around here. I always thought I do pretty well."

The rest of breakfast went on like that. The Joneses always had a good time at meals.

After Juliet had washed the dishes, she said, "Mom, I'm going over to Jenny's. OK?"

"Sure. And you can take them some of that soup I made."

"OK."

"What are you and Jenny going to do?"

Suddenly Juliet had an odd feeling. She had been taught to tell the truth, and quickly her mind tried to arrange things. "Well, I thought we might go out in the woods awhile. And we might pick up some more rocks . . ." she said lamely.

"That's nice. Be careful, though. There might be snakes out. It's about the time of the year for them."

"I'll be careful about snakes, Mom."

When Juliet left the house, her conscience

was bothering her. She picked up a stick and began knocking a stone along the sidewalk. She tried to see how far she could hit the stone without its going off the sidewalk. She kept thinking, *It wasn't exactly a lie. We* are *going to go out in the woods. And I* will *pick up some rocks.*

Still, she felt very unhappy about what she was doing. *I guess I should have told her about the cave—but it's really not a dangerous kind of cave.* This thought did not make her feel any better. Finally she decided just to put it out of her mind.

Jenny White lived with her mother in a little white house on Oak Street. When Juliet went up the front steps, she met Jenny coming out. She had on a knapsack just as Juliet did.

"I'm ready to go," Jenny said.

"Are you bringing anything to eat?"

"Lots. Mom gave us sandwiches and cookies. And I even got a Thermos full of hot chocolate."

"I have some stuff, too. We'll share when we get hungry."

As they started down the steps, Jenny's mother suddenly appeared at the door. "Hi, Juliet," she said.

"Hi, Mrs. White. Oh, I almost forgot to give you this. Mom sent you something." Juliet slipped off her knapsack and took out the plastic container of soup. "My mom made this. It's vegetable soup."

"Why, thank you, Juliet. That was very nice of her. I'm sure we'll enjoy it. Remember to thank your mother for me."

"I will, Mrs. White."

"Now, where are you girls going with your backpacks? Out camping?"

"Oh, just for a hike in the woods," Juliet said.

"Be careful of snakes."

"That's what my mom said. We'll be careful."

As the girls walked on down Oak Street toward the park and the woods, Jenny was frowning. "We didn't exactly tell the truth, did we, Juliet?"

Juliet shifted her knapsack uncomfortably. She saw that Jenny was having the same struggle she was. "Oh, we'll be real careful," she said finally.

Jenny still looked worried. "That's not the problem. I just don't like not being honest with my mom. It makes me feel bad."

"Well," Juliet said after a moment, "I guess I feel the same way. I'll tell you what. Maybe we won't even go inside the cave. We'll just look at it from the outside."

"That would be better."

They reached the park and crossed it. On the way they saw some of the other boys and girls who were in the Oakwood homeschool group. Among them were Flash Gordon in his wheelchair and Chili Williams. They were shooting baskets.

Flash saw them coming and yelled, "Come and play a game!"

"Can't do it, Flash!" Juliet said. "Not now. Maybe this afternoon."

Chili Williams, age nine, was wearing a pair of baggy green shorts and a red T-shirt that had a picture of Batman on it. "Where you girls going?" he asked. "You leaving the country?"

"No, we'll be back."

"I still think it's funny they call him Chili," Juliet said as they went on. "But he does love to eat it."

"He sure does. I believe he'd eat chili for breakfast."

"He does!" Juliet laughed. "He told me once that nothing was better than chili and oatmeal."

"Oh, yuck! I'd just as soon eat dirt."

The two girls reached the thick woods and plunged into its shadows. For a while, they just walked along enjoying the quietness. Once Juliet heard a noise overhead. "See!" she cried. "There's a gray squirrel."

Jenny picked up a stick and threw it toward the squirrel. It came nowhere close to him. He just chattered angrily, then ran along the branch and disappeared. "I guess he's safe from me. I couldn't hit the side of a barn if I was in it," Jenny said.

By and by they came to the dry streambed.

"This is an old riverbed," Juliet said. "Look at the stones here—they're all round stones. That means there was water here at one time."

"I wish it was a river now."

"Why? We've already got Green River."

"I mean a *little* river, where we could just come and sit beside it and wade in it."

"Well, we can go to Green River anytime we want to," Juliet said. "Maybe we can do that next week."

"That'd be fun. Say, I'm getting hungry. Let's stop here and eat something."

"We haven't been out an hour yet," Juliet cried. But then she said, "All right. Just a little something. We want to save enough for lunch."

The girls sat underneath a hackberry tree and ate one cookie each. They swigged some of the hot chocolate. Juliet had brought Diet Coke in her Thermos.

"Diet Coke and hot chocolate. That's almost as bad as chili and oatmeal," she said.

They moved on, and then they came close to the cave.

Juliet said, "We're going to have a stakeout here. Did you bring your binoculars?"

"Right here." Jenny took off her knapsack and fumbled in the bag.

"Good. Now we'll just wait and see if anyone comes."

The girls sat behind some bushes where they could see the cave opening. They watched. They studied the cave with their binoculars. But the only thing they saw, beside the cave itself, was a blue jay. And one time a brown rabbit went by, lazily hopping along. After a while the quiet in the woods became boring.

At last Juliet said, “Let’s just go inside and take a quick look around.” She knew Jenny wouldn’t be happy about doing that. “It’s safe enough, Jenny. There’s no mine shaft in there. Joe and I didn’t see anything scary. Aren’t you curious?”

Jenny was nine years old, one year younger than Juliet. She looked worried again. “Well, I am curious,” she said. “But what if somebody comes?”

“Oh, it’ll only take us a minute.”

“Somebody might already be *in* there!” Jenny protested.

“Then we’ll run.” Juliet was determined to go in. “Let’s leave our knapsacks here. Just take your flashlight, and we’ll see what we can find. If you’re going to be a detective, Jenny, you’ll have to take a chance once in a while.”

Jenny started to do as she was told, but she was still frowning.

The two girls put everything in their backpacks except their flashlights. Then they started toward the entrance of the cave.

As they stooped to go inside, Jenny whispered nervously, "Are you *sure* you want to do this, Juliet?"

"It's all right, Jenny! Nobody's here—it's just like when Joe and I were here before."

Juliet shone her light on the cave wall as they walked slowly along. "Look at these drawings on the wall. Aren't they good? Somebody's tried to make the cave pretty."

Jenny flashed her light about, too. She exclaimed, "They *are* good! I wish I could draw like that! Look, here's a horse, and he's running. Who made these pictures, anyway?"

"There's some more farther in. I'll show you."

The two girls advanced cautiously. Juliet was ready to turn and run if she heard anything. But finally she let out a long breath. "See. It's just like I told you. There's nobody here," she said. "Now I'll show you the backpack."

But the backpack was gone.

"It was right here," Juliet said. She started to run her light around the cave. "See there, Jenny? Whoever it is has made a shelf out of some old wood since Joe and I were here." A few dishes sat on it, and a saucepan, a coffeepot, and most of the cooking things she had seen last time.

"Isn't that a backpack over there?" Jenny asked, shining her light toward the other side of the cave. "It was over there beside the wall all the time."

But Juliet was running her light along the

shelf. “Here’s what I was looking for,” she said. “See what you think of this.”

Juliet picked up the picture, and both girls shone their lights on it.

“Who are they?” Jenny asked.

“I don’t know. That’s what we’ve got to find out.”

“Is there anything written on the back?”

“No. I’ve already looked.”

“Yes, there is,” Jenny said. “It’s in pencil. You can hardly see it, but some writing is there.”

Juliet looked and was suddenly embarrassed. Sure enough, there *was* very faint handwriting on the back of the photo. “I was too nervous last time to look very close. Can you make out what it says?”

But neither of them could read the handwriting.

Juliet said, “Let’s take it outside into the sunlight. Maybe we can read it there.”

Jenny said, “I wouldn’t do that if I were you. After all, it’s not our property. We shouldn’t even be in here. How would you like it if somebody carried off something of yours?”

Juliet remembered saying almost the same thing to Joe. And beside that, she thought of how she would feel if someone found her journal. Suddenly she was ashamed of herself. “That’s right. We’ll just leave it here. Do you think they look alike—the girls in the picture?”

"They do. They look like sisters—or maybe cousins. I'm going to leave, Juliet. I'm afraid."

"Well, you go ahead. You can be the lookout. I want to look around this place a little bit more."

Jenny went outside, and Juliet put back the picture. Then she searched the cave very carefully. She found two old magazines. Then she found a paperback copy of *Tom Sawyer,* one of her favorite books. "So this mystery man likes to read, and he likes *Tom Sawyer.*"

She studied the back of the picture again, but the writing was just too faint to read. "If I could just find a letter with a return address or something like that . . ." she said to herself. But she could not. Then she heard Jenny calling.

When she got to the cave door, Jenny said, "Come on out, Juliet. It makes me feel funny even to be here. It's like messing around in somebody's house."

"Well, all right. But let's watch a little while longer from behind the bushes."

They watched for perhaps another ten minutes.

Then, suddenly, Jenny stiffened. "Look there, Juliet. Who's that?"

Juliet looked in the direction of Jenny's pointing finger. Someone was scurrying through the bushes. Whoever it was, the person was tall and thin and wearing jeans and a red shirt. He had a knit cap pulled down over his ears.

"I couldn't even tell it if was a girl or a boy," Juliet whispered.

"Me either. A boy, I guess. But did you see what he had in his hands?"

"No. What?"

"It was a *rabbit!* Maybe he trapped it."

They waited a little longer, and then Jenny said, "Please. Let's go, Juliet."

"OK. I guess we might as well."

The girls returned through the woods, talking about the mysterious man in the cave as they went. It was Juliet, of course, who said, "Let's come back again Monday—after we get through with our studies and our work."

"I don't know if I want to, Juliet. I don't *like* hiding things from Mom."

"Well, maybe we'll tell our parents," Juliet said. "At least we can tell them part of it—that we found a cave."

"I'd have to tell Mom that much, at least."

"But don't tell her someone's living there."

"Why not? Somebody is!"

"Oh, grown-ups are funny. They might think it was dangerous."

Jenny gave her friend a long look. "They could be right, you know. It *could* be dangerous. You don't know who that was we saw."

But Juliet's mind was made up. "Next Monday," she said firmly, "we'll come, and we'll have a stakeout again."

Sunday School

Juliet Jones loved Sunday school, and she loved her teacher, Beverly Gibson. Miss Bev also was a PE teacher, and she coached the homeschoolers in their softball games. This Sunday she was teaching about the walls of Jericho falling down.

Juliet listened as Miss Bev retold the story.

"And so, you see, there was no way the people of Israel could win the battle. The walls of Jericho were very high. They were strong. They were wide enough to drive a pair of chariots on top."

Billy Rollins was one of those boys who could never be still. He said loudly, "Why didn't they just pull up a big cannon and blow a hole in it?"

"Now, Billy, I think you know there were no cannons in Bible days."

"Well, they had other stuff, didn't they?" Billy argued. He was getting his heart's desire, which was to be the center of attention. He winked at Ray Boyd and asked, "What do you think, Ray?"

"I think they should have had a tank just come and blow a hole in the wall and then drive on in." Ray always followed Billy Rollins's lead, and the two of them made a most obnoxious pair. At least Juliet thought so.

Miss Bev, however, was always patient with Billy.

"I've got a question, Miss Bev." Jack Tanner was a tall ten-year-old boy. His father was going to marry Jenny White's mother soon.

"All right, Jack. What is it?"

"Well, my dad and I—we were reading this story in the Bible last week. And there's a bad woman in this story. You know the one I mean?"

Miss Bev nodded. "Yes. Her name was Rahab. What is your question?"

"Well, this bad woman and her family, they were the only ones that got out alive," Jack said. He had a puzzled look on his face. "That wasn't right, was it?"

"Well, if you read all the story, you know that when Rahab talked to the spies that Joshua sent, she told them she knew that their God was the true God. That was what made this bad woman different from the other people in the city. Can anyone tell me what happened then?"

"I can," Juliet said. "She saved their lives. And they promised that when their soldiers took the city, they wouldn't hurt her or her family."

"Too Smart Jones strikes again!" Billy grinned. He loved to call Juliet Too Smart Jones. Then he said, "What mystery are you trying to solve now, Too Smart?"

Juliet was disgusted. She forgot about being polite. She turned sideways and made a face, rolling her eyes and sticking out her tongue.

"You're ugly enough without trying, Too Smart!" Billy yelled.

"That's enough, Billy. And, Juliet, we don't make faces at people."

"I'm sorry, Miss Bev, but he's just so awful."

Miss Bev said quietly, "We're here to study God's Book, and in this Bible story there's one big lesson. Does anyone know what it is?"

Quiet fell over the room.

And then Chili Williams held up his hand. "I think I know, Miss Bev."

"All right, Roy. What is it?"

"You can call me Chili. Everybody does." Then he said, "Well, there wasn't any way those Israelites were going to get inside and beat those folks. So God did a miracle. He knocked the walls down Himself."

"That's right," Flash Gordon said from his

wheelchair. Usually he went to the church where his father was the preacher. But he and Chili were close friends. Sometimes he came to this church, where Juliet and her family also belonged.

Chili smiled broadly. "When you need a miracle, God can do it."

"You're exactly right, Chili," Miss Bev said. "God can do what we can't do. And He will, when something needs to be done."

"And one of these days you're going to see another miracle," Flash said.

"What's that?" Billy Rollins demanded.

"I'm going to get out of this wheelchair and walk."

The class was quiet. Everybody knew that the doctors had said Flash could never walk again. An accident had badly injured his legs.

"Sometimes we're sure God wants something to happen, but we can't see any *way* for it to happen," Miss Bev said. "That's when we just trust Him to do what needs to be done in the way He wants to do it. That's what's called having faith."

Later, Juliet and Jenny sat together in church. While the announcements were being made—announcements always bored Juliet—she whispered, "Remember. We meet tomorrow and stake out the cave again."

"All right, Juliet. But we've got to tell our

folks that there's a cave there. With somebody in it!"

"OK," Juliet said. "I'll tell my folks, and you tell your mom."

For Sunday lunch, Juliet helped her mother make a delicious salad. Her father always liked bell peppers, and she cut up almost a whole one.

When he saw the salad on the table, he whistled. "Say, now, that's the way a salad ought to be made!"

"I made it just for you, Dad," Juliet said.

Mr. Jones lifted his eyebrows. "You must want something. Every time you're nice to me, I always get suspicious."

"Daddy, that's no way to talk!" Juliet protested. "Can't I be nice just because I love you?"

"Sure, honey. I was just kidding."

Juliet waited until late afternoon before she finally approached her dad about the cave. He had been reading the Sunday papers and had grown sleepy. The papers lay on his chest, and his eyes were almost closed.

"Dad," she said quietly.

"Mmmm—yeah? What is it?"

"Did Joe tell you about the cave we found?"

"Cave? Oh yeah. I think he did say something about it."

Juliet saw that her father was practically

asleep. That was good. "Well, Jenny and I thought we'd just go and look at it again. Will that be all right?"

"I guess that's all right. Be careful, though. Those places can be dangerous." His eyes were closed now.

"We'll be careful, Dad," Juliet said. She kissed him on the cheek and went skipping outside.

There, she thought. *I've told Dad, and he didn't say no. I don't need to say anything to Mom.*

As Juliet came closer to Jenny's house, she thought again of the person living in that cave. *What kind of a man would live in a cave? Is he so poor that he can't afford any kind of house at all? Or not even a room in a motel?*

Then Juliet did what she often did. She began praying. "Lord, I don't know who's in that cave. I don't know if it's a boy or a girl or a man or a woman. But anybody that has to live in a cave is in trouble. So, Lord, I'm asking You to help them . . ."

The Mysterious Cave Dweller

There was nothing that Juliet Jones liked better than to spend time with Delores Del Rio. She loved all the Del Rios—Delores and her brother, Samuel, and the grandparents they lived with. The children's parents both had been circus performers. So had their grandparents. Samuel was eleven, and Delores was nine, but they had learned enough circus acrobatics to put on a good show themselves.

The Del Rio children were being home-schooled, too, with help from several members of the Oakwood support group, including the Joneses.

One of the things that Juliet liked best about visiting Delores and Samuel was that their grandmother was always cooking something good. Today a delicious smell came to Juliet's nose as soon as she entered the house.

"I know what that is," she said. "Your grandmother's making enchiladas, isn't she?"

"That's right. She is. And nobody makes them as good as Grandmother," Delores said. They were still in the hall, and Delores suddenly turned a back flip. "Wheee!" she said. Then she took a bow like a circus performer. "Ta *da!*"

"I wish I could do that, but I'd break my neck."

"And I wish I could do arithmetic problems like you do." Delores sighed.

"Well, you help me learn how to back flip, and I'll help you with your math problems."

The two of them went into the kitchen, where Juliet was greeted warmly by Mrs. Del Rio. She was a small woman with silver hair. She gave Juliet a kiss on the cheek. "Where have you been? I haven't seen you for a week."

"Yes, you have, Mrs. Del Rio. I was over here two days ago. Don't you remember? I ate all the sopapillas you'd made for your husband."

"Oh, I remember, and it's a good thing you were gone when he got home. You know how he loves sopapillas. I think he would have skinned you if he had caught you."

"I may do it now!"

Old Mr. Del Rio came striding into the room just then. He was wearing a white shirt and dark gray trousers. He looked very distinguished with his silvery gray hair. He grabbed Juliet. "I think I'll throw you up through the ceiling and maybe that will stop you from stealing my sopapillas."

Juliet squealed. "Please don't do that, Mr. Del Rio!"

"All right. Not this time. Now you sit down and eat some of these enchiladas." He winked. "I don't want Mama to eat any. She's getting too fat."

"Me, too fat!" Mrs. Del Rio poked her husband in the stomach with a stiff forefinger. "Why, it looks like you're smuggling rice out of China."

Juliet soon found herself filling up on enchiladas and drinking cold lemonade. She sighed. "This is so good."

"You're going to be fat, too," Delores teased. "If you're through eating, let's go upstairs and play dress up."

"Sure." Juliet turned to Delores's grandmother and said, "That was delicious, Mrs. Del Rio. Thank you. I'm practicing making enchiladas and all kinds of Spanish food. But I can't make it as good as you do."

"You haven't had as much practice, Juliet," Mrs. Del Rio said, smiling. "Now you two run along."

The Del Rio attic was filled with trunks and boxes. Many of them contained old clothes. The girls tried on dress after dress and paraded around with out-of-style hats on their heads. There was also jewelry—necklaces, earrings that you fastened on with a screw, and all kinds of rings. In addition to this, there were high-heeled shoes that both girls loved to wear. They admired themselves in an old mirror and then had a tea party.

"Delores, I've got a favor to ask you."

"Sure. What is it?" Delores was wearing a long green dress with sequins all over it. She had to hold up the skirt to keep from tripping over it. She had on green earrings and a hat with big feathers. "What do you want?"

"Well, you see, Joe and I found this cave . . ."

As Delores listened, her eyes grew wide. "Oh, that's neat," she said. "And you really saw the guy that was in there?"

"Well, I don't know if it was a guy. But it was somebody. I *think* it was a guy. So what I wanted to ask you was—Jenny can't go with me today, so I thought you and I could go."

"You want me to help do your detective work? Oooh, that's neat! Sure. Let's go."

"Wait a minute!" Juliet laughed. "We can't wear these dresses in the woods."

"Oh!" Delores looked down at her dress, then at Juliet's. "I guess not." She laughed at herself.

"Wear some grubbies. There are lots of briers out there."

"I've got some jeans. That way I won't get my legs scratched."

Juliet was already wearing jeans and white Nike tennis shoes under her fancy dress. She had on a lime green blouse, and a pair of sunglasses was stuck in her pocket.

As the girls left the house, Juliet picked up her knapsack. "I have binoculars," she said. "Do you have any?"

"No, I don't."

"Then we can take turns using mine. I brought a camera too. It's Dad's old one. And it's got a telephoto lens. See?"

Juliet took out the camera and punched a button. A long tube came out. "It makes everything look close up."

"That's really neat! We can take the cave guy's picture, and then we can take it down to Chief Bender."

"That's what I was going to do. If we get a picture of him, maybe he could put out an APB."

"What's an APB?"

"An all points bulletin," Juliet said, showing off a little. "We'll find out who this cave dweller is," she said.

The two girls retraced the route that led into the park and through the woods. The sun was still high in the sky, and pretty soon both girls were sweating.

"I wish I had on shorts," Juliet said once. "But these briers would scratch my legs to pieces."

"How much farther is it?"

"It's right down this dry riverbed and over to the left. But we've got to be quiet now. If anybody's in the cave, I don't want them to hear us coming."

The two girls moved along as quietly as possible. Finally they were settled behind some bushes not far from the mouth of the cave. The area was wooded, and they could see very little in most directions, but they did have a good view of the cave itself.

Juliet got out her binoculars and handed them to Delores. "Here. You keep watch." She rummaged in her backpack for the camera. "I'm going to be ready to get a picture if he shows up."

The plan was good, but it didn't work very well. The girls sat as quietly as they could for a long time. Then Delores said, "I'm dying for a drink of water."

"We'd better save what we got. I only brought one little Thermos."

"I've got to have a drink. I should have brought some of my own."

"Well, here. Take a little sip, but be careful. We've got to save it."

Half an hour after that, Juliet was stiff from sitting on a rock. She got up on her knees and stretched. Then she said, "I guess he's just not there, and he's not coming. Do you think—"

Delores was peering through the binoculars. "Juliet! There he is!"

Juliet ducked down. She saw someone come out of the cave, and instantly she whipped up the camera. The telephoto lens pulled the person in close, and Juliet gasped.

"Why, it's not a man at all! It's a girl!"

The girl was tall and had long, stringy blonde hair. It was tied with a green ribbon at the back of her neck. It hung down almost to her belt. She was wearing a grubby white sweatshirt, a pair of chinos with a patch on one knee, and black tennis shoes.

"Who *is* she?" Delores whispered.

"I don't know. How old do you think she is? Maybe you can see better than I can."

"Her face is so dirty . . . sixteen, maybe."

Juliet held her breath and watched.

The girl went into the woods, carrying a pan. It was dripping water when she came back. Then she sat down and pulled a handkerchief out of her back pocket. Dipping it in the water, she began to wash her face. She pushed up her sleeves and managed to wash her arms. And then she poured out the water, stood, and looked right in the direction of Juliet and Delores.

Both girls froze.

"She's seen us!" Delores whispered.

"No, she hasn't," Juliet said. "Be still! She can't see through all these bushes."

Sure enough, the girl seemed only to have been watching a blue jay that was fluttering in the tree over the girls' heads. She turned and went into the cave.

There's something sad about her, Juliet thought. *Her shoulders are so slumped. And she looks so tired.*

As soon as the girl was inside the cave, Delores asked, "What do we do now?"

"I don't know. Maybe we ought to go and ask her if she needs any help."

"No! Don't do that!"

"Why not?"

"You just never know. Maybe she has a gun in there. Maybe she's hiding from the police. She's dressed so rough—and why would she be hiding out here if she hasn't done anything?"

"We don't know she's *hiding!* But all right. Let's go home," Juliet said. "I've got to think about this . . ."

They hurried out of the woods. When they came to the park, Delores said, "I'm out of breath. Let's sit down here." She dropped down onto one of the benches. "Is there any more water?"

"No, but there's a fountain over there. You can drink all you want."

They both walked to the nearby drinking fountain and drank thirstily.

"That was good. I was thirsty myself," Juliet admitted.

Then they went back to the park bench and sat for a long time, talking.

All at once Delores snapped her fingers. "I think I've seen that girl before."

"You have?" Juliet was suddenly wide-eyed. "Where?"

"I can't remember where, but I've seen her somewhere. Or maybe it was a picture—like on the post office wall."

"Let's go to the post office and look."

On the post office wall were many pictures of people wanted by the police. But Juliet saw no one who looked at all like the girl at the cave. Most were pictures of hard-looking men.

As they left the post office, Delores said, "Maybe I saw her in the mall. I don't think she's a criminal. She just doesn't look like one."

"I don't think she is, either. And she's so thin—like she's not getting enough to eat."

The two were walking slowly back up the street when Delores said, "Juliet, why don't we ask Joe and Samuel to help? Maybe we can all camp out in the woods one night and do some more snooping."

That was just the sort of idea that suited Juliet Jones. But she said, "I don't think my folks would let us camp out all night. But we could go in the afternoon—as long as we were back before dark. And we could ask Jenny to come, too."

"Sounds good to me. We'll have a great time."

As soon as Juliet got home, she climbed the stairs and stopped at Joe's open door. He was working on something on his desk.

His back was to her, and Juliet sneaked up behind him. She suddenly jumped on him, digging her fingernails into his shoulders. "Gotcha!" she screamed.

Joe let out a yelp that sounded like a wounded lion. He jumped up and knocked over the model he was working on. When he saw who it was, his face grew red.

"You think that's smart to scare somebody half to death? Now you look what you've done to my model!"

"I'm sorry, Joe. I was just teasing."

Joe glared at her. "Well, you can just help me put my model back together again."

"I will, and I've got something to tell you."

Joe looked at her suspiciously. "What is it? Don't tell me you've got another case to solve."

"Joe, Delores and I saw who's living in the cave. Let me tell you about it . . ."

The Big Stakeout

The plan for the big stakeout did not work out exactly as Juliet had hoped. She tried to talk her parents into letting them stay all night, but her father said flatly, "That's out. You're all too young to camp out in the middle of nowhere. Now, if you want to camp in the backyard, that's fine."

Right away Juliet said, "Oh no, Daddy. We'll just go in the afternoon and come back before dark, if that's what you want."

Later, when Juliet explained the plan to Delores and Samuel, she said, "I guess we are a little bit young to stay out all night in the woods by ourselves."

"Not me," Samuel said. "I wouldn't be afraid."

"Me either," Joe said. "I'll bet he'd let just you and me camp out, Samuel."

"No, he wouldn't," Juliet said. "Besides, we're all going to do this together. Anyway, we've got all afternoon to do our stakeout."

"We're going to cook steaks?" Samuel asked.

"No, that's not what a stakeout is!"

"We ought to take some steaks," Joe said. "We can cook them over a fire, and some potatoes, too."

"Why don't we just take napkins and a tablecloth?" Juliet asked.

"That's not a bad idea. I like pink myself." Joe thought he was funny. So did Samuel.

But Juliet just said to Delores with disgust, "I can see that any work that's going to be done, you and I will have to do it."

"I don't have binoculars," Delores said, "but I brought my cell phone. The one I got for my birthday."

"Hey, that's cool!" Joe said. "Now we can call the police or the FBI or maybe even the army if we have trouble with this criminal out there."

"You don't know she's a criminal, Joe!" Juliet said quickly.

"You don't know she's not! Maybe she's a bank robber."

"If she had a lot of money," Samuel said, "she wouldn't be living in a cave, would she?"

Juliet listened to this talk for some time. By now the four of them had gotten far into the woods. She said, "I think we ought to leave most of our stuff here. We can't camp too close to the cave, or she'll see us."

"All right," Joe said. "Let's eat."

"Eat!" Juliet said. "We just got here. You had breakfast an hour ago."

"I'm a growing boy. I need lots of food." He whipped off his backpack and rummaged around in it until he found a package of M&Ms. "Ah, the stuff of life," he said. "How could I live in this wilderness without M&Ms?"

"Give me some!" Samuel said, and the boys began scuffling over the M&Ms.

Juliet said, "When you two get through acting like babies, maybe we can get something done!"

She knew that Joe would be a good helper after the foolishness was over. He loved to be outdoors, and he loved to explore. And she guessed that, really, he enjoyed her mysteries.

Joe, Samuel, and Delores left their backpacks. Juliet took hers because her camera and binoculars were in it. They walked on until they were in sight of the cave.

"There's no sense in all of us watching at once," Juliet whispered. "We'll do it in shifts."

"It's called the watch," Joe told Samuel.

"What's that about a watch?" Delores said, a puzzled look in her eyes.

"The times that soldiers call first watch, second watch, third watch, and so on," Joe said. "This is the first watch. You and Juliet can take that. Samuel and I will go and scout out the territory."

"Well, you might as well go. You're like a worm in hot ashes around here," Juliet said.

"Let me take the phone, Delores. I can call the FBI if you two disappear."

"You're not taking my phone, Joe Jones!" Delores declared.

"OK. I'll just holler for the police. I'll bet if I holler loud enough they could hear me at home."

"Don't you dare!" Juliet said. "I want to find out more about this girl who's living in this cave! If you yell like a wounded animal, she'll hear you."

"I'll get far enough away so she won't hear me. Let's go, Samuel."

Delores was peering through the bushes at the cave entrance. "Do you think she's in there?"

"I don't know. But I brought my camera, just in case."

"Did you get any pictures when you saw her the other day?"

"No. I was too shook up. But I'll get some this time."

The time seemed to drag by, and it got very hot about noon. Then the two boys came back, and everybody sat down to eat sandwiches and apples and cookies.

"Did you see anything while you were scouting around?" Juliet asked.

"We didn't see a thing," said Joe, "but I did

get into the middle of an ant hill. They almost ate me alive."

"I'm sleepy," Delores said. "I'm going back to our camping place and take a nap."

Joe said, "I'm going to explore a little bit more."

"Then I'll stay here and watch with Samuel," Juliet said. She knew that Joe was no good at anything that required patience.

"Why don't we all be back here again in an hour?" Joe suggested.

That was fine with Juliet. "You two go sleep and explore," she said. "Samuel and I will keep a close watch."

She and Samuel started their stakeout. "Here, Samuel. Here are some of Joe's M&Ms."

"Hey, thanks, Juliet. I like M&Ms."

She and Samuel sat watching and eating M&Ms. And absolutely nothing happened.

After a while Samuel said, "This is kind of boring."

"It sure is. But I think a lot of detective work is boring. Sometimes detectives have to sit out in a car for hours just waiting for somebody to come out of a building. And maybe they never come."

"Are you going to be a detective when you grow up, Juliet?" Samuel asked.

"I don't know what I'll be," Juliet said. "Whatever the Lord wants me to be, I guess. Maybe a teacher."

"A teacher! Well, I can tell you, if I ever get out of school, I never want to see the inside of the place again."

"I know, but I really like school. And I like teaching. Sometimes I get to help teach the preschoolers at church, and I always like that."

"Yeah, you're real good with little kids. I've noticed that."

They talked quietly for a while longer. And then Juliet said in a whisper, "Somebody's coming through the bushes!"

It turned out to be Joe and Delores, sneaking back and whispering to each other as they came.

"It's our watch now," Joe said. "Why don't you two go take a snooze?"

Juliet was indeed getting sleepy. "I think I will," she said.

"Not me," Samuel said. "I never get sleepy in the daytime. I'll just stay here with Delores and Joe. You go back and catch a few winks."

Juliet walked back to their camping place. She lay down in the shade there and closed her eyes. She could hear the leaves rustling gently overhead. It was pleasant and cool under the trees.

Soon Juliet felt herself dropping off to sleep, and her last thought was, *I hope she doesn't come while I'm asleep. I want to get her picture.*

Caught!

When Juliet woke up, she was surprised to see that the afternoon was nearly gone. She went back to where the others were watching the cave and found that both Delores and Joe were tired of the stakeout.

"Nothing's going to happen around here!" Joe said. "Delores, let's you and me go for a walk. Let Samuel and Juliet watch the rest of the time. See you two back at the campsite."

As Joe and Delores went off into the bushes, Samuel laughed. "Joe doesn't have a lot of patience."

"Not a whole lot." Juliet shifted around. She seemed to be sitting on a sharp object. She felt around and found a stone.

"What are you looking at that rock for?"

"That's the project Joe and I are doing. Rocks. We're making a collection of rocks."

"I'm collecting birds' eggs. That's a lot more fun. I mean, after all, you see one rock, and you've seen them all."

"That's not true!" Juliet protested. "We have a rock tumbler at home. You put stones in there and turn it on, and it makes them smooth and brings out the most beautiful colors."

But Samuel just grinned. He leaned back and laced his fingers behind his head. "Birds' eggs already have beautiful colors. You don't have to roll them around in a tumbler."

Juliet had taken off her backpack and was using the binoculars again to look at the mouth of the cave. She said, "Don't you feel bad about ending the lives of little birds before they even get started?"

"Don't you feel bad about eating fried eggs for breakfast? After all, they would be chickens one day if you didn't eat them."

"You're as bad as Joe. Every time I feel sorry for a little calf, he says I don't mind eating steaks."

Juliet had always liked Samuel. He was not only a good acrobat, but he was very dependable. Joe would sometimes forget what he had promised to do. But Samuel Del Rio seemed never to forget a promise. She glanced at him and admired his shiny hair and his olive skin. "I wish I had black hair like you," she said.

"You'd look funny with black hair."

"I guess so," Juliet said. "It's funny. People

are never satisfied, are they, Samuel? Whatever we are, we want to be something else."

"Not me," Samuel said. "I'm just what I want to—"

Suddenly Juliet put her free hand over his mouth.

Sitting up straight, Samuel whispered, "What's going on? What is it?"

"Something's going on inside the cave."

"I don't see anything."

"Take the binoculars."

Samuel put the glasses to his eyes. "You're right," he said. "I see it. It's some kind of light. Somebody's in there, all right."

"Come on, Samuel. Let's get up closer. It's going to be dark pretty soon, and we've got to get home before dark."

They inched forward, as quietly as they could. Juliet was careful not to step on any sticks that might make a snapping noise.

At the mouth of the cave, she whispered, "She's got a fire back in there. That's what the light is."

"Yeah. I see it. You want to go in and introduce ourselves?"

Juliet hesitated. She could not help but think that her father and her mother would be totally against anything like that. She could hear them now, saying, "Juliet, you take too many chances. You don't stop and think. Why can't you just be more careful?"

She thought of her parents and their words, words that were sure to come. That thinking kept Juliet standing there in the shadows for a minute or two longer.

But the flickering firelight inside the cave was just too tempting. "Come on, Samuel," she whispered. "It won't hurt just to get a little closer."

"OK, but be ready to run. She might have a knife or even a gun."

Juliet led the way. There were no flashlights this time. Trailing her fingers along the worn rocks that formed the cave wall, she felt her way toward the flickering light. Closer and closer they came, their sneakers making no noise on the floor of the cave. And then Juliet stopped. She nudged Samuel with her elbow.

Sitting beside the fire was the girl that Juliet had seen earlier. Her knees were drawn up, and she had her arms wrapped around them. Her hair was not tied up this time but flowed down her back. The only light was the light of the campfire, but Juliet could see one side of her face clearly. She was staring into the flames.

Again there was something about the girl that touched Juliet. She could not tell what it was, but there was a sadness about the girl that made Juliet feel very sorry for her.

"What's she doing?" Samuel whispered.

"Shhh."

The girl got up from the fire and took something from the shelf. Now she stood looking at it.

Juliet straightened up with surprise. *It's the picture,* she thought.

And then the girl began talking. She seemed to be talking to the photograph.

Maybe if I can get a little closer, Juliet thought, *I can hear what she's saying.*

She motioned to Samuel to stay where he was. But just then he must have shifted his feet and stepped on some loose stones. Suddenly there came the rattle of rolling rocks.

Juliet froze, but the girl spun about. Quickly she bent over and picked up something. As she straightened, Juliet saw by the flickering light of the fire that she held a small ax. The firelight glinted on its steel blade. And then the girl started toward where Juliet stood in the shadows.

Juliet whirled. She started to run toward the entrance of the cave. She ran right into Samuel.

He went down flat on his back.

Juliet whispered desperately, "Get up! Hurry! She's got an ax!"

This seemed to help Samuel make up his mind very quickly. He scrambled to his feet, and they felt their way toward the cave door, hurrying as fast as they could.

Juliet could hear the footsteps behind

them. They seemed to be getting closer, and fear swept over Juliet. *Why did we ever come here?* she thought wildly. *She's going to chop us up with that ax!*

The two detectives burst out into the late afternoon sunlight and rushed into the woods.

"You're forgetting your backpack!" Samuel gasped.

"I'll come back and get it later. Just run, Samuel!"

They dove through the brush. Branches swept across Juliet's face and burned like fire. Briers grabbed at her clothes. Vines tripped her as they fought their way through the thick undergrowth.

"Who are you, and what are you doing here?"

The voice of the girl reached them, but Juliet did not think it was the time to stop and answer. "Just run, Samuel!" she cried again.

"What do you want?"

The voice continued to call, but neither Juliet nor Samuel stopped to have a conversation.

By the time Juliet and Samuel reached a small clearing, they seemed to have escaped the girl. They both slowed down enough to catch their breath.

"I got a stitch in my side," Juliet said.

"That's better than having an ax in your head. Did she *really* have an ax?"

"Didn't you see her?"

"No. I don't have eyes in the back of my head!"

"Well, she had one, and she was coming right after us!"

Samuel began to rub his face. It had a deep scratch on it. "We've got to keep going. She could catch up with us yet."

"What about my backpack? I can't leave my backpack."

"There's nothing in there worth getting tomahawked for," Samuel said.

Juliet knew that was true. "All right," she said. "Let's go tell Joe and Delores."

They took a roundabout path back to their camping place.

Delores saw them coming through the bushes. "Is something wrong?"

"We nearly got tomahawked by a wild woman," Samuel said. His eyes were bright. Now that the danger was over, he seemed to be excited about the whole thing. "We went right into the cave, and we saw her."

Joe acted miffed at having been left out of the action. "What was she doing?" he demanded. "And how come you went into the cave? Why didn't you wait until we all got there?"

"We saw a fire, and we just thought we'd go see what she was doing," Juliet said.

"Well, what *was* she doing?"

"She was looking at that picture that we saw. And then she started talking to it."

"Talking to a picture!" Delores said. "What was she saying?"

"I don't know. I couldn't get close enough to hear. And then Samuel stepped on some rocks and made a racket, and she heard it. And then she picked up the ax."

"Wasn't my fault," Samuel defended himself. "The rocks were just there."

"I wasn't blaming you, Samuel. It could have been me just as well." Juliet took a deep breath. She noticed that her hands were not steady yet. "It was pretty scary," she said. "And I had to leave my backpack."

"You did? I'll go back and get it," Joe said at once.

"No, Joe! Don't go back there!" Juliet cried, but it was too late. Joe was already gone, running at full speed.

"I wish he wouldn't do that," she said. "Nothing's in that knapsack that I have to have right now."

They waited. And waited. And then Samuel said, "Here comes somebody. I sure hope it's him and not that ax carrier."

It was Joe, and he held the backpack high. "I got it! I got it!" he cried.

"Did you see her?" Delores asked.

"Didn't see anybody. I just crawled up, grabbed the bag, and ran. Fast as I could."

"Well, let's get going," Juliet said. "Thank you, Joe, for going back for my knapsack. That was dangerous. But I sure would hate to lose all my stuff."

The four of them tramped back to town, and everybody was somewhat subdued. They talked very little except that, from time to time, somebody would make a comment on what the next step should be.

Juliet did not really know *what* the next step should be.

She and Joe said good night to Samuel and Delores, and they headed toward the Del Rio house. Then Juliet said, "I'm so tired I can hardly stand up."

"Getting scared does that to you." Joe grinned, then said, "Tell me again about the girl."

"I felt sorry for her, Joe."

He stopped dead still. He grabbed Juliet by the arm and demanded, "You feel sorry for somebody who was trying to hit you with an *ax?*"

"Well, I think she was scared. If I was out there all alone in a cave, and if I heard somebody creeping in, *I'd* use an ax to defend myself —if I had one."

"I guess I'd do the same thing," Joe admitted.

The two trudged on. As they turned up the street toward their house, Joe said, "How much of this do we want to tell Mom and Dad?"

"I don't know. And it's got me worried."

"Well, *they* sure would worry if they knew you were having anything to do with a girl carrying an ax! And you weren't supposed to be in that cave, anyway!"

"Let's just don't say anything tonight. Then we'll talk to them later, Joe. Maybe tomorrow."

"OK. It's your case, Too Smart."

Juliet was too tired even to fuss at Joe for using the nickname she hated.

At home, they found that their parents had gone out to visit friends. Their mother had left a note on the kitchen table, saying, "You can find your supper in the oven. If we happen to be a little late, just go to bed at your usual time."

A wave of relief swept over Juliet. *I won't have to talk to them tonight at all,* she thought. *But I know I will, sooner or later.*

Juliet found the leftovers, and she and Joe ate hungrily. Afterward they sat around and watched a video.

Then Joe said, "I'm going up and work on my invention."

"I think I'll just go to bed and read and relax."

Joe turned and grinned at her. "Well, being a detective is pretty exciting at times. A little bit too exciting for you today, I bet."

Juliet smiled, but her heart was not in it. "I think you're right, Joe."

Much later, just before going to sleep, Juliet lay in bed thinking about the happenings of the day. As usual, she went over things again and again in her mind. She could hear a dog barking in the distance, and she glanced toward the bedroom window. She wondered whose dog it was.

Then she began to pray, and her prayer tonight was mostly for the girl in the cave. "I don't know who she is, Lord, but she needs a friend. She's bound to be scared and lonely, and I'm asking You, Lord, to help me be some kind of help to her." Then she said, "And, Lord, I haven't been honest with Mom and Dad about all of this. That was wrong, and I'm sorry. Please forgive me. And I promise that I'll tell them everything."

That made her feel better, and finally Juliet began drifting off into sleep. Her last thought was, *I've got to talk to that girl—without scaring her to death. How can I do that? Maybe I could just walk up to the cave, whistling . . .* Here Juliet's thoughts broke off, and she floated into sleep, warm and secure in her bed.

The Girl by the Creek

"I'm never going to get into this kind of a mess again, Joe. Never."

Joe looked up from his desk. He was wrestling with his math problems again, and a furrow wrinkled his brow. "What kind of mess are you talking about this time?"

Juliet was doing a paint-by-number picture of George Washington. Carefully she put a dab of paint on the canvas and looked at her work with satisfaction. "I mean trying to hide things from Mom and Dad. I should learn pretty soon."

Joe made a face. "That was about as upset as I've ever seen Mom get."

Juliet and Joe had had a big conference with their parents the day after her adventure at the cave.

"I guess she had a right to be. That time in the cave could have been bad."

"But it turned out all right. I don't see why they had to ground us."

"Well, it wasn't a *long* grounding. We can be glad for that." Juliet sighed. Then she dipped the brush into the paint again and carefully applied it to George Washington's face.

Over the past three days, she had thought a lot about the girl in the cave. But she had not come up with any way to help. Once she had thought, *I'm just going to give up. It's none of my business anyhow.*

But she still felt sorry for the girl, whoever she was. She was sure that there must be some great trouble in the girl's life, and she could not stop thinking about her.

Joe kept frowning at his math book. He said, "I don't know why they have to put these problems into words. Why don't they just put down two plus eight equals blank? I can always do those."

"Let me see." Juliet went to his desk and read the problem. She shook her head. It was as clear as day to her. Patiently, she began explaining it to him.

As she was in the middle of doing this, the door opened, and their dad stepped in. "And what are you two up to this morning?"

"I'm trying to work these dumb old problems!" Joe said. "I don't see why I have to do all this. I'm not going to be anything that needs numbers."

"Everybody needs to understand something about numbers, Joe. What are you going to be? An animal trainer maybe? An acrobat?"

"Aw, Dad! I'm going to be an inventor. You know that."

"Well, inventors have to learn how to think clearly. Joe, I used to have the same kind of trouble with numbers that you're having." Mr. Jones sat down at the worktable and grinned at his son. "I had trouble for at least a year or two. And then, one day it just all came to me. I think there's such a thing as being ready to understand certain things."

Juliet said, "I heard the same thing about learning to read. Until somebody's *ready* to learn to read, there's not much you can do about it. Then when they do get ready, you can't stop them."

"Well, I'm ready for numbers," Joe said, frowning at both of them. "It just won't come."

Their dad sat and talked for a while longer. Then he said, "Since you're not grounded anymore, what are you going to do this afternoon?"

"Take us fishing, Dad. We could have a great time."

"That'll have to be tomorrow. I've got to go make a bid on a job this afternoon."

Mr. Jones supervised building bridges and skyscrapers. Sometimes he took a job a long way off, and Juliet and Joe missed him a lot.

Lately, his work had all been close to home and family, which his children liked. Getting up from the table, he said, "Tomorrow we'll take the boat out to the lake and catch all the fish you want."

"Then I guess we'll just fool around this afternoon," Juliet said.

"That's the most fun of all—just fooling around. And stay out of trouble now, you hear? Don't go back to that cave! I don't know who that girl is, and I don't want you out there by yourself."

It was on the tip of Juliet's tongue to ask her dad to go with them. She could always come to him for help, and she thought he would not mind helping this time. But since he had to be gone this afternoon, she put it in the back of her mind to ask him later. "All right, Dad. It'll be fun going fishing tomorrow."

Early in the afternoon, when their work was done, Juliet said, "Let's go look for some more rocks, Joe."

"Suits me. Anything's better than arithmetic or chores."

Ten minutes later, when they were ready to leave the house, Joe said, "We've already looked along the creek. Let's go over toward the river this time."

"Sounds good, but that's a long way. We'd better take along something to eat."

"Good," Joe said. "Never can have too much food is my motto."

When they left on their rock hunting expedition, their pockets were stuffed with candy and peanut butter sandwiches.

Juliet and her brother had a wonderful time exploring the woods on the north side of town. It felt good to be out of the house. They even found a few rocks.

Joe complained once. "We've already found almost all the kind of rocks there are around here. Maybe we can get Dad to take us out to Arizona or Colorado somewhere."

"That would be neat! We could go skiing in Colorado."

"You couldn't ski."

"How do you know I couldn't ski?"

"Because you can't even roller-skate worth anything. Not like me. I'm an expert."

"Joe, you brag too much!"

"Well, some baseball player said, 'If you can do it, it ain't bragging.'"

"I don't care what some old baseball player said! Bragging sounds awful. You sound just like Billy Rollins."

"Oh no! Not him! I'll have to watch what I say, then. Anyway, maybe we can go to Colorado for a vacation. I bet we could learn to ski. Even you. Even Mom and Dad."

They must have walked for two miles on the north side of town. Then they came to a little creek that bubbled along within its banks. Both Juliet and Joe loved water, and they spent some time making boats out of sticks. There was a path along the creek, too, and they followed it for a while, throwing rocks into the water as they went.

Juliet knew that the creek would join the river later on, but Joe said, "It's too far to go all the way to the river. Anyway, I already found this one special rock. I don't know what it is. I'll have to look it up in the book when we get home."

They came to a narrow place in the creek just then. As they did, Juliet saw someone on the other side.

Instantly she stopped and stiffened. *It's the girl,* she thought. *It's the girl in the cave.*

The girl was kneeling to get a drink. And then she looked up.

Juliet could see her clearly for the first time. She had ash blonde hair, and she was very pretty.

The girl jumped up, and Juliet was sure she was about to run away. Quickly Juliet called, "Hello there!"

The girl looked past them, perhaps to see if they were alone. But there was no one else to see. She stood stiffly where she was, and finally she said, "Hello."

"We've been out collecting rocks," Juliet said.

After a moment, the girl said, "What for?"

"Oh, we're just making a collection of all different kinds," Joe said. "For school."

Juliet could tell he had guessed that this was the girl from the cave. She said, "We live over in town, but we come to the woods a lot." She hesitated and then asked, "Do you live close to here?"

The girl hesitated, too. "Not far," she said cautiously. "Well, I've got to go now."

"Wait a minute," Juliet said. She was thinking fast. "Before we left home, we stuffed our pockets with stuff to eat. Some of it's beginning to melt. You'd be doing us a favor if you'd help us eat it."

For a moment Juliet thought that the girl still was going to leave them.

But something about the invitation must have caught her interest. She was very thin and had hollow cheeks. Maybe she was hungry. She swallowed hard. Then she said, "Well, if you're not going to eat it yourself . . ."

"No, we aren't. Here, Joe. Let's see if we can get across the creek without falling in."

They began crossing on rocks that stuck above the surface of the water.

On the other side, Juliet began to empty her pockets. "Let's sit down," she said. "We can have a picnic."

"Yeah," Joe said. "It's always a good time to have a picnic."

He pulled out a package of M&Ms. "Here. I got four packages of these." He handed one of them to the girl. "Do you like M&Ms?"

"Yes."

"Before we start on M&Ms," Juliet said, "let's eat these peanut butter sandwiches. Then we can have the M&Ms for dessert."

"Well, I've got Snickers bars for dessert," Joe said, emptying another pocket. He grinned happily. "Nothing like Snickers bars for dessert."

When they began eating the bread and peanut butter, Juliet saw that the girl was indeed very hungry. She started to eat slowly, but then she tore into the sandwiches with such obvious hunger that Juliet could hardly bear to watch her.

"I don't think I can eat this," Juliet said, looking at her own sandwich. "Maybe you could eat it? I'd just throw it away."

"No, I'll eat it," the girl said quickly.

Handing over the sandwich, Juliet said, "My name's Juliet Jones. This is my brother, Joe." She waited, but the girl was stuffing bread and peanut butter into her mouth.

There was a short silence as the girl chewed on her sandwich. She kept looking at them. Then she said, "I'm Molly Jackson."

"I'm glad to know you, Molly. There's some Jacksons that live in town."

"Yeah," Joe said. "That's Henry Jackson and his family. Are you related to them?"

"No. No, I'm not."

Both Juliet and Joe tried hard, but neither of them was able to find a way to make Molly Jackson talk.

The girl finished off all the bread and peanut butter and started to get up. "Well, I've got to go now. Thanks for the sandwiches—and the candy."

"Oh," Juliet said, feeling in her pocket. "Look what I still have." She brought out a bag of gummy bears. "I don't much like these things," she said. "Do you?"

"Neither do I," Joe said. "Do you like them, Molly?"

"Well, yes, I do . . ."

"Then you take them, but be careful. They're real gummy."

Juliet watched Molly Jackson get ready to leave. "If you're going our way, maybe we can walk a little way with you," she suggested.

For a moment she was sure that the girl would say no. She had smears of chocolate around her mouth and a cautious look in her eye. She still appeared to be very nervous.

But Molly Jackson finally said, "Well, all right. But I've got to get home soon. So I'll have to move right along."

They followed the creek to the highway, and Juliet and Joe did most of the talking. Molly seemed to listen, but she rarely said anything.

When they came to a side road, Molly said, "Here's where I turn off. I've got to go now. Thanks again for all the food."

Juliet didn't want their meeting to end like this. She felt sorrier than ever for the girl. Now that she knew her name and saw how hungry she was, Juliet's heart went out to her.

"Are you in a *real* big hurry, Molly?"

"Well, yes. Sort of," Molly said cautiously.

"Could you sit down just for a minute? I want to talk to you about something."

"Talk about what?"

Seeing that the girl was not going to sit down, Juliet went on. "Well, it looks to me like you need a little help."

"I don't need any help!"

"Most people do," Juliet said. "I know I've needed help lots of times."

"Me too," Joe said. He sat down on an old fallen tree. "Everybody needs help. Anybody as hungry as you are sure needs help."

Juliet was sure Joe's thoughtless words were going to make the girl angry and drive her away. Quickly she said, "Molly, the Bible says that a friend loves at all times. If you do need help, Joe and I would like to be your friends."

Without warning, tears formed in Molly Jackson's eyes. Her lips quivered, and she turned her back to them. Juliet saw her shoulders shaking, and she put an arm around her. "It's OK to cry," she told Molly. "I do it myself."

Molly did not answer for a long time. When at last she turned around, tears were running down her cheeks.

Juliet took out a handkerchief and gave it to her. She said, "Here. Sit down. You can tell us about it. If it's a secret, we won't tell anybody if you don't want us to. Honest."

Molly Jackson looked very young and frightened. Maybe she just didn't know what else to do. But without another word, she sat down on the log.

Juliet held her breath a second as she took a seat beside her. She knew she could not pry information out of Molly. She just hoped that the girl was ready to talk.

"I do need friends," Molly said. Her voice was very low, and she twisted the handkerchief Juliet had given her. "I've been living in a cave near here."

Juliet almost said, "I know you live in a cave," but she didn't. She thought that could come later. Instead, she asked, "Why are you living in a cave? Are you maybe running away?"

"Yes. That's what I'm doing—but I haven't done anything wrong!"

"Why don't you just tell us about it, Molly?" Juliet asked quietly. "Sometimes it helps to talk."

"I suppose it can't do any harm. You see, after my parents died, they took my sister and me and put us in different foster homes. The people I was living with wouldn't let me talk to my sister at all."

"What's your sister's name?" Juliet asked.

"Sarah."

"How old is she?"

"She's seven now. I'm seventeen."

Molly reached into her pocket and pulled out a picture. It was the one that Juliet had seen. "This is Sarah and me before our parents died."

"She's pretty. She looks a lot like you."

Molly laughed. "I'm so dirty I look like a pig. I couldn't be pretty."

"I think you are," Joe said. It was probably the first time he had ever told a girl that she was pretty. He must have surprised himself, for his face got red and he said, "I mean under all the dirt."

"Joe, don't be impolite!"

"No. He's right. I *am* dirty. I've been living in that old cave, and I'm dirty. And I'm about to starve to death."

"Did you run away from your foster home?"

"Yes, I did, Juliet."

"Were they mean to you?" Joe asked.

"No, it wasn't that. But I found out that Sarah had written a letter to me, and they hid it from me. Well, I happened to find it and saw the postmark on it. And it was from a place near Oakwood. So I ran away so that I could get to see my sister."

"What would you do if you found her?"

"I'll be eighteen next week!" she said eagerly. "And then I can get a job and take care of Sarah myself—if I can just get her."

"I think you ought to come home with us," Juliet said.

"Home with you! I can't do that!"

"Why not?"

"Why—your *parents!*"

"We've got the best parents in the world," Joe said. "They'll help anybody."

But Molly Jackson kept on shaking her head. "I just couldn't do that. I'll get along someway."

It was plain to Juliet that Molly was afraid, and she knew that the girl was half starved.

Juliet and Joe Jones often disagreed, but not this time. They both threw themselves into the job of persuading Molly Jackson to come home with them.

But Molly said, "Your parents would call the police right away. They could list me as a vagrant or a runaway."

"They wouldn't do that," Juliet said.

"Anyway, even if they did, we've got a good police chief. His name is Bender. He's an Indian."

"I'm afraid of police. I'm just afraid that someone will take me back to that foster home. I love my sister so much, and I'm so unhappy where I am without her."

It took a long time, but finally Juliet and Joe convinced Molly that it was safe to go and talk to their parents.

"Just talk to them," Juliet said. "You're going to love our parents, and they'll love you, too. And I'll bet they'll know what to do to help. They always do."

Molly Jackson shook her head one more time. "I don't see how that could be, but I'll go see them anyhow. I've gone about as far as I can on my own."

"It'll be all right," Joe said. "God can do anything."

Molly gave him a straight look. "You think that *God* cares?"

"Why, sure I do!" Joe said with astonishment. "The first song I ever learned was 'Jesus loves me; this I know for the Bible tells me so.'"

"Just come, Molly. We can talk about it on the way," Juliet said. She did not want Molly Jackson to change her mind.

And soon the three of them were headed straight for the Jones house.

Parents to the Rescue

"Mom—Dad, this is our new friend. This is Molly Jackson. Molly needs help. We thought you would know how to help."

Neither Mom nor Dad showed even a trace of surprise as Juliet introduced the newcomer. Juliet was never more proud of her parents than at that minute, for Molly was scruffy looking indeed. She was wearing faded blue jeans, ripped at both knees, and a man's shirt, far too large for her.

And then Juliet saw that Molly was unable to speak. "Molly's had a bad time," she explained. "But you always know how to help people. So we thought we'd bring her to you . . ."

"I see," Mrs. Jones said. "Perhaps it would be a good idea to clean up a little. Then we'll have something to eat. And then we'll talk."

Soon Molly was in the downstairs shower.

Juliet said, "Mom, she hasn't any clean clothes to put on . . ."

"I know that. Let's you and I quick go into my closet and pick out some things. I've an extra pair of jeans that might fit. And we'll find her a shirt and some underwear. And shoes."

That's what they did. Then Juliet cracked open the bathroom door and slipped the clean clothes inside.

While Molly showered, Juliet helped her mother finish making the meal.

In the middle of the preparations, her father came into the kitchen. "Is this the girl that was in the cave, Juliet?"

"Yes, it is."

"Did you go back there? You know what I told you."

"No, Dad. I promised you I wouldn't. And I didn't. We didn't go near the cave. We went way over toward the river. Joe and I were looking for rocks for our collection," Juliet explained. "And we just ran into her by accident. And we started talking."

Mr. Jones frowned. "Well, who *is* she? She looks half starved—beside being scared to death."

"I think she is both," Juliet's mom said. "She seems to need help all right."

"Let's hear her story first. Then we'll know better what kind of help she needs."

"She's real jumpy, Dad. But I'll get her to

tell you what she told us. And then you can figure out a way to help her."

When Molly Jackson came into the kitchen, she looked entirely different. Mrs. Jones's clothes were a little large for her, but they were neat and clean. She rubbed her hand on the shirt sleeve, murmuring, "It's good to have clean clothes on. And to get a shower. Thank you so much."

"You are welcome," Mrs. Jones said. "Now, come, let's eat. And while we do, we can talk."

Juliet and Joe and their dad were ready to sit at the table.

"Why don't you sit right there by Juliet, Molly?" Mrs. Jones suggested.

As soon as they were all in their places, Mr. Jones smiled and said, "Time for the blessing." He bowed his head and prayed, "Father, we thank You for this food, and we thank You for this guest. We ask Your blessings on her. In Jesus' name. Amen."

Mrs. Jones had planned a good supper. They had fried potatoes with onion and green pepper, baked pork chops, green beans, rolls, and chocolate pie.

Juliet noticed that the candy and peanut butter sandwiches had not dulled Molly's appetite. She also noticed that Molly used very good table manners. She was glad when no one began to ask questions right away. Instead, everybody talked about things that went on around the house and around the town.

Molly Jackson said almost nothing.

"I helped Mom make this chocolate pie, Molly. See if you like it," Juliet said.

"Oh, it's so good! I've always loved chocolate pie."

"What about if we go into the rec room and sit down and relax? I need to rest after all this food," Juliet's dad said.

As soon as they were in the recreation room, Joe said, "Do you play Ping-Pong, Molly?"

"I used to."

"I'll play you a game."

"Oh no. I don't think so."

"Aw, come on," Joe said. "It'll be fun."

"Watch out for him. He's a shark," Mr. Jones warned.

As it turned out, Molly was too good a player for Joe. She beat him soundly. But when he challenged her to another game, she said, "No. That's enough for me."

They all sat down then, and Mr. Jones looked at Juliet.

She knew at once what he wanted. "Molly, why don't you tell Mom and Dad just what you told us?"

Molly bit her lip and looked at Mr. and Mrs. Jones with something like fear again. And then she began to tell her story.

"I was wrong to run away, I suppose," she

finished, "but I'm so worried about my little sister."

Juliet's father then began to ask questions. He asked Molly where she was from. Louisiana. He asked the names of her foster parents. Fred and Ethel Bellew. He got their phone number. Then he asked, "And why are you staying in the cave, Molly?"

"Well, it's a dry place. And private. And I didn't have any extra money. I know that Sarah is around Oakwood somewhere—and that's why I'm here."

"Well, have you done anything about finding her?"

"I went to the library to find out what I could about the town where my sister's letter came from. It's not far from Oakwood. The name of it is Rogers."

"Yes, Rogers is less than an hour away. And what's the name of your sister's foster parents?"

"I don't know. And I've been afraid to ask questions. I might get caught and sent home again." Molly sat looking down at her feet. When she looked up, she lifted her chin. "I'm eighteen next week," she said. "As soon as I'm eighteen I can get a job and take care of Sarah myself."

"Well, we'll have to see about that," Mr. Jones said. "There'd be some legal questions to settle."

"You can do it, Dad," Juliet cried. "You know how to do things."

"One thing's for sure, Molly, " Mrs. Jones put in. "You can't go back to that cave. It's just too dangerous staying out there alone."

"I know. I've been scared two or three times. Just the other day, somebody came right into the cave. I ran them off with an ax."

Juliet suddenly knew it was time for a confession. "That was us, Molly. I'm sorry."

"You!" Molly stared at her with amazement.

"We knew someone was living in the cave, and I just wanted to find out who it was." Then Juliet told her story. When she was through, she said, "I'm sorry if we scared you, but—"

"Well, you scared Juliet and Samuel too," Joe said. "They told me about the ax."

"I would never use it unless I had to protect myself."

"I'm sure you wouldn't," Mrs. Jones said. "But you mustn't go back there again."

"You may need to stay with us for right now," Juliet's father said.

Tears rose in the girl's eyes. Her lips trembled, and she could not speak for a moment.

Then Mr. Jones said, "I think what we'd better do first is call Chief Bender."

"The police!" Molly cried. "That's what I don't want! They'll arrest me."

"No, it's not a matter of arresting anybody. But we've got to face up to the facts. And we've got to start by finding your sister. The chief can help us."

Juliet took her hand. "It's all right. Chief Bender's a nice man."

"I'll go make the call," her dad said. "Don't worry about it, Molly. It's going to be all right."

The call was made, and within half an hour Chief Bender called back. When Mr. Jones hung up the phone, he said, "Your foster parents have not made out a missing persons report, Molly."

"I'm not surprised. They didn't really care much about me," Molly said.

"I can't understand that," Mrs. Jones said sadly.

"They weren't ever mean to me," Molly said. "They just didn't seem to care much for anybody."

"Anyhow, the chief spoke to the welfare people. And since you're going to be eighteen in a week anyhow, I think we're going to get custody of you until then."

"Hey, that's cool, Molly!" Juliet cried. "I always wanted a big sister, and now I've got one."

"Yeah, having a big sister is great!" Joe said. He grinned broadly. "Now you can do all the woman stuff in the kitchen, like washing the dishes and stuff like that. And I won't have to."

Molly Jackson looked around at the Jones family. She could not get a word out. But finally she swallowed hard and said, "I never knew anyone could be so kind."

Some Real Cool Detective Work

"You look great, Molly!" Juliet said. She was getting dressed, and she'd turned to see that Molly Jackson had put on the blue dress that her mother had given her. It just fit Molly, and so did the new shoes that Juliet had helped her pick out. "You look really nifty!" Juliet exclaimed.

"I . . . I feel funny. I haven't worn real clothes in so long that I'd almost forgotten what it was like."

"Well, you look good, that's for sure. Let's go. I hear Dad starting the car. He always likes to be early."

"I hope people don't start asking me a lot of questions at church."

Juliet saw that Molly Jackson was still not over her fear. "You won't have to answer any.

We'll just tell everybody you're a friend of ours from out of town. And you are."

When they went downstairs, they found Mrs. Jones and Joe waiting for them.

"Hurry up," Joe told Juliet. "You know how Dad is about being late to anything."

"He's very punctual," their mother agreed. "You look so nice, Molly."

"Thank you, Mrs. Jones. Thanks for the dress—and the shoes and everything. You've been so good to me."

When they got into the car, Mr. Jones said, "Hang onto your hats! Here we go!"

Joe, who thought his father should buy a sports car instead of keeping their eight-year-old Chevrolet van, said, "Don't worry, Molly. This thing won't break any speed records."

"Don't you speak of this car that way. It's paid for!" his father said. But then he laughed. "One of these days we'll get a fancy one, Joe. Wait and see."

When they got to the church, Juliet saw that everyone was looking at their visitor. Several of her friends, including Helen and Ray Boyd, came up and asked, "Who's that?"

"Oh, just a friend of ours from out of town. Her name is Molly."

"She's so pretty," Helen said.

"Yes, she is."

Several people greeted the Joneses' visitor. Juliet watched Molly to see how she was taking all the attention. The girl seemed nervous at first. But finally, when they were seated, she drew a deep breath. "That wasn't so bad," she said.

The organist began playing, and the choir came in.

Molly leaned over and whispered, "My mom and dad always took Sarah and me to church every Sunday."

"Oh, I'm glad to hear that!"

Molly picked up a songbook and turned the pages. "I'll bet I know every one of these songs."

She seemed to, for—no matter what they sang—Molly's clear voice rose. She did not even look at the book sometimes. Juliet knew most of the songs by heart, too, but she could not sing as well as Molly.

After church, they drove back home and had a great dinner. They had beef roast, potatoes, carrots, salad with honey mustard dressing, and then homemade apple pie.

"My mom's the best cook in the world," Joe said.

"Yes, she is. I taught her everything she knows about cooking, and she does well," his father said with a straight face.

"Daddy, you couldn't cook an egg!" Juliet protested.

"I could if I wanted to. I just don't like to show her up."

"You couldn't any more cook a meal than I could build one of those bridges you're always building," Mrs. Jones said. She looked over toward Molly. "You must think we're crazy, always teasing each other like this."

"No," Molly said, smiling and shaking her head. "I like it. It's the way a family ought to be."

After the meal was over, the table was cleared, and the dishes were washed and put away. Then they all found their way into the living room. They watched the news for a while. But then Mr. Jones picked up the remote and turned off the TV. He settled himself into his easy chair and said, "Now we're going to do something that Juliet will love."

"What's that, Dad?" she asked eagerly.

"We're going to play detective. Get your notebook, Juliet, and keep track of everything that's said."

Juliet knew that her father was teasing her, but she didn't care. She jumped up and grabbed a notebook and pencil from the table by the wall. Then she came back and said, "Ready."

"Now, Molly, I'm going to ask you all the questions I can think of. And then anyone else can ask questions. Somehow we're going to find out where your sister is."

The questions and answers went on for a long time but seemed to get nowhere. And then it was Juliet who had an idea. "Molly, do you still have that letter your sister sent you?"

"Yes. It's upstairs with my things." Joe had gone to the cave for Molly and brought back what few belongings she had.

Molly got up from her chair and went upstairs. Soon she returned with the letter. "But there's no return address," she said.

Mr. Jones frowned at the envelope. "And no name, but maybe I can figure out something . . ."

"Maybe we could get a lawyer," Joe said helpfully.

"And that's an idea. Not to help with the letter, but—as a matter of fact, I might even ask Ted Stanfield about it." Ted Stanfield was the lawyer that Mr. Jones's construction company used.

Juliet made a note that her dad should talk to Mr. Stanfield. When she looked up again, she saw Molly looking at her. "It's going to be all right, Molly," she said. "We're going to find Sarah. Don't you worry."

Later that afternoon, Juliet and Joe took Molly with them to the park. When they got there, they found many from the homeschool group busy playing. Billy Rollins was there along with Flash Gordon and Chili Williams. Samuel and Delores were there along with Jack Tanner. And, of course, the twins Helen and Ray Boyd were there. And Jenny White.

"We're going to have a horseshoe pitching

contest," Billy Rollins announced. "And I'm going to win."

Flash laughed at him. "You always think you're going to win, but you never do."

"I'm going to win this time," Billy bragged.

"I bet you don't," Samuel Del Rio said.

"You just be careful, Samuel. You're talking to a world championship horseshoe pitcher."

"I know what," Juliet said. "Let's have a tournament."

"How are we going to do that?" Helen Boyd asked. "You always want to boss everything."

"It'll make it more fair. Like, I mean, I'll play against you, Helen, and Ray can play against Jenny. Then the winners of those two matches will play each other. And then . . ."

That was pretty much the way it went. The tournament started, and Juliet beat Helen without any trouble. Setting up another match, she said, "Why don't you play Billy, Molly?"

"Hey, no fair! She's a grown-up!"

"You're not afraid of a girl, are you?" Chili Williams asked. "I'll play you, Miss Molly."

"All right, but I haven't had much experience with this game."

It appeared that Molly had natural ability at horseshoes, though. She beat Chili Williams.

The contest continued until finally the only two people left were Molly and Flash Gordon.

"All right, Miss Molly," Flash said. "You

might run faster than I can, but I'm going to beat you this time."

The game was very close, but at the end, with one ringer, Molly won the tournament.

"Hooray! You win, Molly!" Juliet said.

Most of the kids cheered and congratulated her.

Then Juliet said, "The winner buys ice cream for everybody!"

"But I don't have any money," Molly whispered.

"I do," Juliet said. "Dad gave me some."

At the ice cream parlor, everyone chose his own favorite ice cream.

"What do you like best, Molly?" Joe said. "I like rocky road."

"I like pistachio."

"Yuck! That's green! It makes me sick!"

Nevertheless, Molly got pistachio, and everybody made a great deal of noise. They kept it up until the owner had to tell them to leave.

On the way home, Molly said, "I wish I'd had good friends like you do, kids. It must be wonderful."

Juliet thought about that for a while. Then she looked at Joe. "That's right, isn't it, Joe? We *have* got lots of friends, and we forget to be thankful for them."

"When Sarah and I get together, we're going to find boys and girls just like you, so Sarah can have lots of friends."

"And you too, Molly," Joe said.

"And me too." Molly smiled. She put her arms around them both and hugged them, saying, "I sure am glad you dug this hermit out of her cave."

The Great Dog Wash

And so we have decided to divide all our home schoolers into teams." Mrs. Winfred Boyd was talking, and the collection of students stared at her suspiciously.

Mrs. Boyd was very thin and very proud. She also was sure that she could organize people better than anyone else in the world. Today's meeting was for all the homeschooled youngsters in the Oakwood area.

"Uh-oh!" Juliet murmured. "We're in trouble now!"

"What can she do to us?" Joe asked.

"She can do awful things. Don't you remember some of the projects that she's gotten us into?"

"Oh yeah!" Joe mumbled. "I forgot."

Mrs. Winfred Boyd beamed. "I'm sure you haven't forgotten that the fund raising for our trip to Washington, D.C., must be completed by this week."

"Oh my!" Juliet whispered.

"What's wrong? Did you swallow your gum?" Flash Gordon asked. He leaned forward in his wheelchair to look at her face.

"No, I didn't. But with everything that's been going on, I did forget all about the fund raising."

"I think the least the parents could do is to pay for the trip." The whisperer this time was Billy Rollins. "It's our one big field trip for all year." He added, "I volunteered to be in charge of the whole group. A bunch of kids like you aren't to be trusted on a trip like this."

"I don't think there's going to be a trip," Chili Williams said. "Last I heard, there wasn't enough money to get us halfway to Washington."

Mrs. Winfred Boyd frowned at all the whispering. "May I have your attention, please!" She waited until all was quiet, and then she beamed again. "Now I'll read who is on each fund raising team. And we are expecting each team to get out and raise money for our trip."

"How are we going to raise the rest of the money, Mrs. Boyd?" Jenny White asked.

"Well, ordinarily we would help you. But we feel that all of you need to learn responsibility. Therefore, each team is going to do everything on its own. *You* will decide what money must be raised, *you* will decide how to do it, and the winning team will receive a prize."

"I'll bet I know what the prize will be, too," Chili muttered. "A box of Cracker Jacks with a tin ring in the box."

Mrs. Boyd was still talking. "Now we will break up into groups, and you will immediately make your plans to raise money. Remember, a prize for the winners!"

Juliet looked at the paper that Mrs. Boyd had handed her. She saw that she was on team number six, along with Flash Gordon, Chili Williams, and Jenny White. "Let's get at it," she said. "I guess we've got to do something about this."

Their team went outside and walked slowly along the sidewalk. Flash cut some wheelies in his wheelchair. Then they stopped under a towering oak tree to talk things over.

"Anybody got any great ideas?" Flash asked.

"I do," Chili said, grinning. "I think we ought to just hitchhike to Washington. We'll get there quicker that way than we ever will by trying to raise money."

"Oh, we'll get the money somehow," Juliet said crossly. She was still upset with herself because she had forgotten the fund raising. She really wanted to go to Washington and see all the things that she had read about—the Washington Monument, the Lincoln Memorial, the White House . . . "So," she said, "any ideas? I mean *good* ideas."

"We could bake cookies," Jenny said.

"That's no good." Juliet shook her head. "Everybody's going to bake cookies. That's what everybody does to raise money."

"Yeah, even the Girl Scouts," Chili said. "How about a car wash?"

Flash shook his head on that. "Those that won't be baking cookies will be washing cars. We've got to find something that nobody else is going to do."

They stood looking at each other. They stood for a long time without thinking of anything.

At last Flash said, "I believe I could think better if I had a milkshake."

Chili Williams said, "I believe I could think better if I had a bowl of chili."

Jenny White laughed. "I believe I could think better if I had a Coke."

Juliet frowned. "You're just trying to get out of thinking! But maybe it wouldn't be a bad idea. Let's go down to the ice cream shop for some cones."

Juliet, Jenny, Chili, and Flash soon found themselves in a booth at the ice cream shop, enjoying their favorite ice cream.

When they were almost finished, Juliet glanced out the window. She was still thinking about raising money. Now she saw Chief Bender go by, leading one of his bird dogs. The chief was a bird hunter.

"I've got an idea," Juliet said.

"Let's have it."

"Why don't we do a dog wash?"

"What in the world is a dog wash?" Jenny asked.

"You know how people hate to give their pets baths. Well, we could wash their pets for them. Why, I bet we could get enough pets to beat every other team."

Chili said, "I never heard of a dog wash, but it might work."

"It's something new. And it's different," Flash said. "How do we do it? And where do we do it?"

"I'll tell you," Juliet began. "Here's what we'll do . . ."

"We'll never get all these critters washed!"

Juliet looked at the dogs lined up in the empty building they were using for their dog wash. They had gotten the place free because the mayor himself owned it, and he was glad to help. Juliet had even gotten the newspaper to run a free ad.

By ten o'clock this morning, the day her team planned having the great dog wash, they had at least thirty dogs of all sizes and shapes. Juliet had been happy at first. But now, two hours later, her hands were puckered and red, and she was sick of washing dogs.

"We're never going to get them all washed this way," Chili said.

"I agree," Flash added. He was washing a Chihuahua, and he held up the dog with one hand. "If they were all as easy as you, little fella, it would be easy. No hair, and you're no bigger than a rat."

The Chihuahua snapped at Flash's fingers, but the boy laughed at him. Then he dried the little dog and said, "Well, there's number seventeen, but look at this pack we've got to go."

"We're making money," Juliet said, "but I don't think we'll last at it."

"We're never going to get them all washed this way," Chili repeated.

But they did.

Then, at the very last moment, when all the dogs were washed and the owners had picked them up, Juliet looked up to see Henry Davis coming in. He was being pulled along by four enormous dogs.

"Man, those are the biggest dogs I ever saw!" Chili breathed. "What are they, anyway?"

Henry Davis heard the question. "These are Saint Bernards. Fine animals, aren't they? Little bit hard to wash, though. I was glad to see your ad in the paper."

Juliet swallowed. She was truly sick of dogs. She wished that Henry Davis had never showed up. But she smiled. "There's an extra charge for real big dogs like these, Mr. Davis."

"I'll pay double," Mr. Davis said. He handed the leashes over to Juliet. "These are real calm and friendly dogs. Won't give you any trouble at all. Well, I'll be back in an hour."

After Mr. Davis left, Juliet and her teammates stared at the four dogs.

"I don't see how we'll ever do it," Flash said. "We don't even have a tub big enough for these monsters!"

"All right, Too Smart Jones," Chili said. "Time to be too smart. How are we going to get these critters washed?"

Juliet glared at him. She hated that nickname. "We'll just have to wash them."

"They're bigger than we are," Jenny protested. "We can't even pick one up and put it in a tub."

Juliet grew still, and her eyes grew narrow.

"She's thinking!" Chili cried. "I know that look! She's thinking!"

Indeed, Juliet was thinking. She was tired of dogs, and so was everyone else. But something had to be done. Suddenly she slapped her hands together. "I've got it," she said. "It won't take five minutes for all four of them."

"Aw, come on now, Juliet," Chili said. "It takes longer than that to wash one of them little weenie dogs."

Juliet sniffed. "You just bring the dogs.

You'll see." She kept the leash of one of the Saint Bernards and gave one each to everyone else.

"Where are we going?" Flash asked.

"I'll show you," Juliet said. "It's right around the corner."

The huge Saint Bernards tugged at their leashes. They all made quite a sight as they paraded down the street.

Flash had the most fun of all. His dog was pulling him along in his wheelchair. "I need to get a harness for her!" he cried with delight. "This is fun!"

"It's fun, but I don't see no dogs getting washed," Chili said gloomily.

"Well, you will," Juliet answered. She was proud of herself for thinking up such a good idea. She said, "Now, look. You see that? There's the answer."

Her three teammates looked across the street at Acme Car Wash.

Silence settled over the group. Two dogs sat down on the sidewalk and began scratching fleas.

Finally Jenny said, "You mean we're going to take them through that?"

"Why not? It washes cars," Juliet said.

"Whoopee!" Flash yelled. "But have you got any money?"

"Sure. I have what the people have paid us. All we have to do is lead the dogs in there."

"We'll get sopping wet," Jenny protested.

"We're already sopping wet," Juliet said, "and we're getting paid double. Come on."

Juliet marched up to the car wash. She stood before the machine that took the coins, saying, "Get ready. We can do them all at the same time."

They lined up the four dogs.

"Everybody ready?" Juliet asked.

"Ready," said Flash.

"All ready," said Chili.

"I guess so," said Jenny.

The dogs were very quiet. Two of them sat down to scratch. The other two looked around as if they were bored.

Juliet dropped the coins in the slot. Almost at once, water began shooting out of the nozzles above them. All four children and all four dogs were instantly soaked.

Juliet's scheme might have worked except for one thing—the Saint Bernards had never been in a car wash before. They were frightened out of their wits. All four leaped forward, braying in deep voices.

"Hold on there!" Juliet yelled to her dog. The big animal paid her no attention at all. She felt herself being dragged through the car wash. Then she heard other voices crying, "Stop!" "Wait up there, boy!" "Wait for me!"

All four dogs were off and running. They shot out from the other end of the car wash, and Juliet thought it was over. But the dogs were still scared out of their senses. They split up and ran in four different directions.

Chili's dog carried him straight into the open door of the barbershop, where he scared the daylights out of two barbers and four customers.

Jenny's dog pulled her half a block and then into the candy store. He dragged her around the counters, knocking over candy displays. Then he ran out, leaving Jenny sitting in the wreckage.

Flash had more trouble than the rest. Although he tried to put on the brakes of his wheelchair, it made no difference to the dog. She pulled him down the street, while he bounced up and down and tried to keep the wheelchair from tipping over. Then his dog ran right into the fountain in the middle of the square.

Juliet was determined to hang onto her Saint Bernard, but she knew she could not hold on for long. The dog came to the police station just as Chief Bender opened the door.

"What's going on?" the sheriff shouted. Then he was knocked backward by one hundred fifty pounds of wet fur and muscle. Suddenly Sheriff Bender was all tangled up in the leash. He and Juliet and the dog landed in one muddle on the station floor.

The chief separated himself, got up, and then looked down at Juliet.

"I don't know what you call this, Too Smart Jones, but it's even worse than some other things you've pulled."

It took a while, but Juliet's team finally got the dogs safely back and dried. They were exhausted by the time the day was over.

But when all the students met with Mrs. Boyd, she counted everyone's money and announced, "The winner is team six! Come and get your prizes, boys and girls."

The prizes turned out to be four boxes of Cracker Jacks.

Happy Ending

Juliet Jones took a lot of teasing about the great dog wash. In fact, she became so thoroughly sick of the subject that she even snapped at her dad when he teased her about it.

"Daddy, I wish you'd never mention that dumb dog wash again!"

Looking surprised by Juliet's sharpness, her father turned. "Why, honey, I thought you did great. You have more imagination than any ten people I know. Now all you kids will get to make the trip to Washington. And I get to be one of the sponsors, and we'll have a great time."

Juliet hugged her father. "I know. I'm sorry I'm so crabby. I guess I'm still worried about what's going to happen to Molly."

"Well, we've prayed about that. And we're doing all we know to do to settle the matter."

"I know that, too. And I do believe God's going to help us find Sarah and put her and Molly together. But . . ."

Juliet's father had kept her up-to-date on what was happening with the problem of Molly and Sarah. Mostly, he had turned the matter over to the lawyer that did the legal business for his company.

Juliet and her dad were still sitting outside in the porch swing when the phone rang. Right away Mrs. Jones brought out the portable phone, saying, "It's for you, dear. I think it's Mr. Stanfield."

Joe and Molly came out, too. Everyone had been waiting for news of what was going to happen next.

Taking the phone, Mr. Jones said, "Hello. Yes . . ." There was a long silence, and then Mr. Jones said, "Thank you. I'll be at your office soon."

He turned the phone off and then turned to face his audience.

"Well, don't just sit there," Mrs. Jones begged. "What did he say?"

And then a smile appeared on Mr. Jones's lips. He waved the phone around. "It's all going to be all right. Molly, they've found your sister."

Juliet jumped up and grabbed Molly. The two of them danced around the porch. Then

Joe joined them, and all three danced. Even Mr. and Mrs. Jones hugged each other.

Finally there was enough quiet for Mr. Jones to say, "The guardianship papers are filed, and Sarah's foster family wants to meet you, Molly. Now, from what I understand, they want to keep your sister. But they also would like you to come and live with them, too—if that's what you'd like."

Tears ran down Molly's face.

Juliet hugged her again and whispered, "I told you it was going to be all right, Molly. This is the way God does things."

"We'll go to see the family tomorrow. They'll be expecting us."

The Chevy van moved along the streets slowly as Juliet's dad looked for the house. Their forty-five minute drive from Oakwood had been an anxious time all the way. In spite of what Mr. Stanfield had said, there was always the chance that something could go wrong.

"I'm so nervous," Molly said. "What if they don't like me?"

"Don't be silly! They'll love you."

"There it is. Three-oh-four." Mr. Jones pulled up in front of the house.

Juliet got out of the car, saying, "Come on, Molly. I think this is going to be your new home."

Molly climbed out, and then her eyes went to the house. "Sarah!" she cried.

All the Joneses watched as Molly Jackson flew across the yard. She snatched up the little girl who came running to meet her.

And Joe said, "Well, I guess this is one case that you really solved. Good detective work, Too Smart."

Soon they were all inside, getting acquainted with the Smiths. Mr. Smith was a tall man with a pair of warm blue eyes. His wife was friendly, too. And they seemed very glad, indeed, to meet Molly.

"I kept writing you, Molly," Sarah said, "but you never wrote back."

"I never got your letters, Sarah. It's a miracle that I'm here now."

"Well, this is like a storybook ending," Mr. Smith said. "We never had any children, and now we've got two fine daughters. That is, if you will stay with us, Molly. We'd love to have you."

Mrs. Smith got up and put her arms around Molly. "We surely would. There's a community college here. You can go to that—study art, if you want to. We've heard about your art ability. We'll help you any way we can."

The Joneses were invited to stay for lunch, but Mrs. Jones whispered to Juliet's dad, "It's a family thing. Let's let them get acquainted."

"You're right," he said. "We'll come back another time and visit. And Molly has already promised to come and visit you, hasn't she, Juliet?"

"She said she'll come to our next home-school program."

When it was time to leave, Molly hugged Juliet so hard that she squeezed the breath out of her. "Juliet Jones, you are the greatest," she whispered. Her eyes were damp with tears, but they were tears of happiness. "I'll be coming over with Sarah, and we'll watch your school program. All right?"

"I'm so glad you've got a home, Molly."

Ten minutes later the van was whizzing down the road.

Juliet Jones was happy. "I like happy endings," she said to Joe, who was sitting beside her and staring out the window. "Did you hear what I said? I like happy endings."

"I was just thinking of a new invention."

"What is it?" Juliet asked, not thinking.

"An automatic dog washer," he said.

Mr. and Mrs. Jones overheard this from the front seat. They began laughing.

Juliet started to get angry, but then she saw the twinkle in Joe's eyes.

"Well, that sounds better than some of your other inventions. I'll even help you with it. Then maybe we could make a boy washer."

Juliet reached over and pulled Joe's hair.

He dug an elbow into her ribs. They struggled for a while, then just fell into laughter as the van rolled down the highway.

Get swept away in the many Gilbert Morris Adventures available from Moody Press:

"Too Smart" Jones

4025-8 Pool Party Thief
4026-6 Buried Jewels
4027-4 Disappearing Dogs
4028-2 Dangerous Woman
4029-0 Stranger in the Cave
4030-4 Cat's Secret
4031-2 Stolen Bicycle
4032-0 Wilderness Mystery

Come along for the adventures and mysteries Juliet "Too Smart" Jones always manages to find. She and her other homeschool friends solve these great adventures and learn biblical truths along the way.
Ages 9-14

Seven Sleepers - The Lost Chronicles

3667-6 The Spell of the Crystal Chair
3668-4 The Savage Game of Lord Zarak
3669-2 The Strange Creatures of Dr. Korbo
3670-6 City of the Cyborgs

More exciting adventures from the Seven Sleepers. As these exciting young people attempt to faithfully follow Goél, they learn important moral and spiritual lessons. Come along with them as they encounter danger, intrigue, and mystery.
Ages 10-14

Dixie Morris Animal Adventures

3363-4 Dixie and Jumbo
3364-2 Dixie and Stripes
3365-0 Dixie and Dolly
3366-9 Dixie and Sandy
3367-7 Dixie and Ivan
3368-5 Dixie and Bandit
3369-3 Dixie and Champ
3370-7 Dixie and Perry
3371-5 Dixie and Blizzard
3382-3 Dixie and Flash

Follow the exciting adventures of this animal lover as she learns more of God and His character through her many adventures underneath the Big Top. Ages 9-14

The Daystar Voyages

4102-X Secret of the Planet Makon
4106-8 Wizards of the Galaxy
4107-6 Escape From the Red Comet
4108-4 Dark Spell Over Morlandria
4109-2 Revenge of the Space Pirates
4110-6 Invasion of the Killer Locusts
4111-4 Dangers of the Rainbow Nebula
4112-2 The Frozen Space Pilot

Join the crew of the Daystar as they traverse the wide expanse of space. Adventure and danger abound, but they learn time and again that God is truly the Master of the Universe. Ages 10-14

Seven Sleepers Series

3681-1 Flight of the Eagles
3682-X The Gates of Neptune
3683-3 The Swords of Camelot
3684-6 The Caves That Time Forgot
3685-4 Winged Riders of the Desert
3686-2 Empress of the Underworld
3687-0 Voyage of the Dolphin
3691-9 Attack of the Amazons
3692-7 Escape with the Dream Maker
3693-5 The Final Kingdom

Go with Josh and his friends as they are sent by Goél, their spiritual leader, on dangerous and challenging voyages to conquer the forces of darkness in the new world. Ages 10-14

Bonnets and Bugles Series

0911-3 Drummer Boy at Bull Run
0912-1 Yankee Belles in Dixie
0913-X The Secret of Richmond Manor
0914-8 The Soldier Boy's Discovery
0915-6 Blockade Runner
0916-4 The Gallant Boys of Gettysburg
0917-2 The Battle of Lookout Mountain
0918-0 Encounter at Cold Harbor
0919-9 Fire Over Atlanta
0920-2 Bring the Boys Home

Follow good friends Leah Carter and Jeff Majors as they experience danger, intrigue, compassion, and love in these civil war adventures. Ages 10-14

Moody Press, a ministry of the
Moody Bible Institute, is designed for education,
evangelization, and edification. If we may assist you
in knowing more about Christ and the Christian
life, please write us without obligation:
Moody Press, c/o MLM, Chicago, IL 60610.